The Green and the Red

A Angela,
en espérant que
cette lecture la
fera sourire et
ouvrira son appétit,
Armand.

The Green and the Red

A Novel by Armand Chauvel

Translated by Elisabeth Lyman

Ashland
Creek
Press

The Green and the Red

A Novel by Armand Chauvel

Translated from the French by Elisabeth Lyman

Published by Ashland Creek Press

www.ashlandcreekpress.com

ISBN 978-1-61822-030-1

Library of Congress Control Number: 2013948248

Printed in the United States of America on acid-free paper.

All paper products used to create this book are Sustainable Forestry Initiative (SFI) Certified Sourcing.

For Yara Dutra

One

Léa scanned the menu desperately in search of an escape route. She'd come to Paris for the day expecting to meet with her high school classmate at the bank where he worked. Instead, he'd suggested they discuss her request over lunch at a traditional brasserie on Boulevard Saint-Germain.

There was a pizza on the menu, but the prospect of picking out all the bits of ham by hand didn't hold much appeal. It was a relief, then, when she spotted a goat-cheese salad among the starters.

"We're out of goat cheese," the waiter told her.

She bit her lip and looked back down at the menu. The lunch service was in full swing, and her old classmate, whom she hadn't seen for ages, had ordered a steak and was now devouring their complimentary basket of potato chips. At length, she made her choice.

"I'll have the mixed-greens salad with ham and crudités, but without the ham." The waiter raised an eyebrow, then went away, leaving her face-to-face with Jean-Claude's silk tie and questioning look. "Uh … I'm allergic to ham," she mumbled, embarrassed.

Were there any known cases of ham allergy? Perhaps not, but it was only a partial lie. Ham truly disgusted her, especially now that she had a pet miniature pig named Charline. Jean-Claude, who was gifted with neither tact nor perceptiveness, began describing his boundless passion for Iberian acorn-fed ham, a delicacy he treated himself to every time he went to Spain.

"You should put that on your menu! It'd be a hit."

Visions of pigs' legs hanging in an outdoor market came to Léa's mind. Maybe it was because the way they were lined up made her think of chorus girls in a music-hall show, but after a while they'd started to look like human legs to her. But Léa's trouble with meat had begun much earlier. When she was ten, her grandparents had given her a baby chick. She raised it lovingly until the day her father, noticing her charge's robust health and thick plumage, transformed it into a chicken potpie. Although she'd seemed to have gotten over this early trauma fairly quickly, the incident had left its mark.

Jean-Claude looked her straight in the eye. "To be honest, I never would've imagined you as a restaurant owner. Or living way out in Rennes."

Nobody would have imagined her as a restaurant owner (or chef—she was also the one working the stove). A brilliant student, she'd graduated from high school with honors at the age of sixteen. That was when things had gotten a bit messed up: She began fine arts studies, but it took her four years to realize that art wasn't her true calling. She found herself unemployed and without a degree, much to her parents' dismay. Jean-Claude was only assuming what everyone else had—that she'd botched things up. Another handful of chips went down the hatch.

"An organic restaurant, too!" he added, giving her a strange look.

He could disparage organic food all he liked, she thought,

as long as he didn't catch on to the rest. She now regretted not lying outright and describing La Dame Verte as a restaurant serving traditional fare. Thanks to her ridiculous scruples, she now found herself on thin ice. At stake was a loan of fifteen thousand euros—a crucial amount if she was to stay in business.

The waiter appeared with the steak and salad. "Since you didn't want ham, we gave you tuna."

"Huh?" She paled but immediately grasped that if she didn't want to give herself away, she had only a half-second to recover. "Well, then! Thank you very much."

She began to imagine how surprised Jean-Claude would be—and the chain of events that would ensue—if, heaven forbid, she were to leave the fish untouched.

Another allergy?

Actually, I'm a vegetarian.

Ve—vegetarian?

At that point, the jig would be up, and she could forget about the loan. What bank would be crazy enough to finance a vegetarian restaurant? And even imagining that Jean-Claude were an open-minded, eco-conscious, New Age banker, she wouldn't be able to avoid that same tired old line of questioning.

Ah! But I thought vegetarians ate fish.

Nope.

Not even teeny tiny mini-shrimp?

Have you ever seen fish growing in a garden? she would retort, ignoring his attempt to annoy her. *Or seafood sprouting from tree branches?*

From the way he beamed as he carved up his steak, it was clear that Jean-Claude was a die-hard carnivore. *But what about some nice foie gras sautéed with chanterelle mushrooms?* he would probably say next, in the discussion playing out in Léa's mind. *Or baked duck with olives? Or stewed rabbit? Not even a roast chicken?*

The argument that would follow might vary slightly in the details, but it would generally go something like this: He would ask if she had any nutritional deficiencies, and she would say no, she was very healthy. He would reply okay, fine, but people have been eating meat since prehistoric times, and without meat in our diet, our brain would never have reached its current size. She would inform him that it was not the eating of meat but the invention of cooking—which increased the energy we could extract from food and thus freed us from constantly searching for calories—that led our brains to grow bigger than those of our ape-like ancestors. Try reading a few science magazines, she would add.

He would get worked up and protest that humans were at the top of the food chain. Léa would tell him that this idea wouldn't have convinced the early Christian martyrs in the lion's dens. He would assert that like any other animal, man was a predator and had the right to take his prey. She would compliment him for placing people on the same level as animals; after all, did we not share 98.7 percent of our genetic code with the bonobo and 95 percent with the pig?

This comparison of human and non-human animals would irritate Jean-Claude even further. He would accuse her and her ilk of preventing people from enjoying their food with their moralizing talk about animal suffering. Anyway, could she show him scientific proof that it doesn't hurt carrots to pull them out of the ground? She would challenge him to locate the carrot's central nervous system—he could win a Nobel Prize! He would ask what she would do if her plane crashed in the Andes mountains and all she had to eat was a can of pork and beans. Vegetarianism wasn't a religion, she would reply—just a life choice—and she wouldn't refuse to make an exception if extreme circumstances warranted it. She would then point out that the meat industry was destroying the environment. He would call her an extremist and claim that she cared more about battery hens than starving children. Showering him with facts and figures, she would establish the direct connection between the meat industry, the over-exploitation of agricultural resources, and world hunger.

Finally, out of arguments, Jean-Claude would go back to nutritional deficiencies and say that vegetarians had low sex drives because they didn't get enough vitamins. Yes, she would agree, they were all pale, anemic, and impotent—just look at the hundreds of millions of vegetarians living in India. Exasperated, he would remind her that Hitler didn't eat meat. Correct, just like Tolstoy, Leonardo de Vinci, and Einstein, she would counter. He would accuse her of being under the influence of a guru and continue along those lines until she stood up and smacked him on the face. It didn't take much sometimes.

She stuck her fork into a piece of tuna, which was undoubtedly contaminated with mercury. In any case, from her long experience, she knew that nobody gave up meat just because of a conversation. There had to be a certain predisposition, plus a triggering event or lucky coincidence. As with Paul McCartney, who was eating lamb one day when he looked out the window and saw some young sheep capering around in a meadow. But that wasn't all. In Léa's view, vegetarianism was to food what love was to sex. The same relationship existed between a greasy hamburger and a terrine of grilled vegetables with arugula pesto and grilled almonds as between a porno movie and *Romeo and Juliet*. Would Jean-Claude agree? His plate looked like a battlefield. A mound of green beans had resisted all attacks from his fork, while some distance away, a piece of bone and a few chunks of fat lay in a pool of blood. She half-expected him to order steak tartare for dessert. And she wondered what he would think if he were to try the rice-milk, white almond butter, and medjool date panna cotta she served at La Dame Verte. Most people had no idea of the nutritional benefits or exquisite flavors vegetarian cuisine had to offer. The catch was that if Jean-Claude ever came to her restaurant, he would see how empty it was, and ... good-bye, fifteen thousand euros. No—she needed to be patient, clever, and tolerant. And then, wiping the red juice from his lips with a napkin, Jean-Claude really went and did it.

"Nice and rare, just the way I like it. Seriously, I don't understand those vegetarians. Gotta be stupid."

Two

Was Mathieu in love with Astrid Nedelec, or was it just a case of strong sexual attraction? He had just answered the fourteen questions of the True Love Test, which he'd found in a magazine, and the result seemed incontestable.

I would be deeply despondent if she left me. Hard to say, since they hadn't yet slept together, but he supposed so. On a scale of one to nine, he'd give this a five.

I sometimes feel I am obsessed with her; I can't think of anything else. Yes, he was obsessed with her, but more physically than otherwise. Three out of nine.

Making her happy brings me joy. He liked working with her, but no, he wouldn't get up at night to get her a hot-water bottle. Two out of nine.

I would rather spend my time with her than with anyone else. Of course—at least in Rennes, where he didn't know anyone. Three out of nine.

I'd be jealous if I thought she was interested in someone else. Nine out of nine. He was still a human being with feelings, after all.

I long to know everything about her. Let's not get carried away. She was intelligent, but not very imaginative or interested in many things. Three out of nine.

I desire her in every way—physically, emotionally, and mentally. Physically, yes; emotionally, yes, but only because of his involuntary solitude. And mentally? He didn't get it. Again, three out of nine.

I have an endless need for affection from her. Chéri, his grandmother's Chihuahua, came to mind as someone who had an endless need for affection. Two out of nine.

She is the perfect romantic partner for me. The word *romantic* made him uncomfortable. And anyway, he couldn't answer until he had slept with her. For now he would put five out of nine.

I feel my body responding when I'm close to her. Nine out of nine—physically, Astrid was his type. Just shaking her hand put him in quite a state.

She's constantly on my mind. By playing with the words a bit, he could have put nine out of nine, since work was always on his mind, and the two—his work and Astrid—were inextricably linked, but that would have skewed the results. Two out of nine.

I want her to know everything about me—my thoughts, fears, and desires. Yikes! A slippery slope that could lead to marriage. One out of nine.

I eagerly look for signs of her desire for me. He wasn't looking for anything, but he was quite pleased by the obvious interest she showed. He was even pretty sure that she'd left her ex because of him. Five out of nine.

I become very depressed when there's a problem in my relationship with her. He wasn't a sociopath, so as a matter of course, he preferred to maintain a good relationship with everyone. Five out of nine. That made a total of fifty-seven points. Even adding ten points to make up for the cynicism inherent to the male condition, he was still far from the maximum score of 126.

A jolting of the train shook him from his thoughts, and he noticed that they were approaching Montparnasse station. The first-class car was full of top executives from Rennes who, like him, were traveling to Paris for the biennial international food innovation trade fair. Mathieu tried to imagine how they would rate on the True Love Test and wondered how they would react if he were to speak to them about his problem with women. Problem? He went to the restroom to freshen up. In the mirror he saw a man with broad shoulders, dark hair, brown eyes, and a large and slightly crooked nose—the kind of imperfection, he thought, that distinguishes you from ordinary mortals. He was brimming with testosterone and, despite having always had an active sex life, he'd never had the slightest technical difficulty in bed. And Astrid Nedelec, the communications director and daughter of the big boss, was infatuated with him. So … what problem?

At the trade fair, Jean-Sylvain, Astrid's cousin, had already arrived at the Nedelec Pork stand and was briefing the stand attendants. That's the trouble with family businesses, Mathieu thought. The roles aren't well defined, and a young and inexperienced financial officer can stick his nose anywhere he wants. Mathieu sighed and went over to shake his hand.

"I'm looking for Astrid," he said.

"She's late again," replied Jean-Sylvain coldly.

Was it because of his great height that this moron looked down on everyone? Jean-Sylvain didn't have so much to be proud of, Mathieu thought. His main strong point—the only one, in fact—was his ability to pinch pennies. Exhibit A: the jackets that were too short for him and the abominable cheap colognes he was always drenched in. In any case, Mathieu had no desire to spend any more time than necessary with this rookie.

Mathieu went off to explore the aisles of the trade fair. The competition had outdone itself this year: sprayable olive oil, squirtable cheese, wine jellies, deer-testicle chewing gum, Tex-Mex tripe, morel mushroom butter, and other amazing things. One thing was sure—he loved the agrifoods industry. It was a dynamic and innovative sector, and he was a highly imaginative workaholic. When he'd left Paris to become category manager at Nedelec Pork in Rennes, the company was producing only fresh sausage, smoked and unsmoked ham, andouille sausage, dried sausage, and traditional white sausage. Excellent products but a bit outdated, and distributed without any real strategy. In his first six months there, Mathieu had boosted sales in large and medium-sized supermarkets and, trespassing on the marketing director's territory, proposed the creation of a garlic-flavored cocktail sausage. And bingo! The cocktail sausage was a hit at stores all over France. Fabrizia, the marketing director, was thanked and shown the door. Mathieu was given her job and the never-ending resentment of Jean-Sylvain, who'd had almost as much of a crush on the pretty Italian woman as Mathieu did. He thought back wistfully to Fabrizia's devastating smile, her high-heeled boots, and the rivalry between them that did not preclude a certain attraction.

His cell phone rang, putting an end to his reverie.

"Hello, Mathieu!" The silky voice belonged to Astrid. Her meeting at Bill & Burton, their PR agency, was likely to take longer than expected, and a crew from the local news station would be stopping at their stand at eleven o'clock to film a short segment. She didn't know if she would get there in time. "Would it make you nervous to be on camera?" she asked.

"Are you kidding? My backup career plan was to become a game-show host."

She broke out laughing. "You men and your delusions of grandeur!" Then she took on a more serious tone. "But you have to be careful, you know. This isn't *Questions for a Champion*. The media can be real sadists sometimes."

"Don't you worry about a thing."

"Okay, great. If I'm not there in time, marketing gets interviewed and no one else."

He could have kissed her. What she meant was that Jean-Sylvain, the cousin she cherished almost as much as he did, was not to be allowed near the microphone. Mathieu headed back toward the stand, whistling a little tune, but stopped in his tracks when he caught sight of Auguste Nedelec's colossal frame towering over the crowd. Oh, no! What was Astrid's dad doing there? Wasn't he supposed to be taking a week off because of his health problems?

"Astrid will be furious, but I couldn't resist. I jumped on the first train," Auguste announced with a jovial smile that thrust his wide chin forward.

Mathieu realized the interview had just slipped through his fingers. Damn it! Not to mention the additional market share the chief executive officer was about to make them lose. Although he had masterfully transformed a modest butcher shop in downtown Rennes into a prosperous family business, Auguste wasn't exactly a stellar spokesperson. Mathieu nevertheless felt affection for this self-made man, workaholic, and … his future father-in-law? He admired the patriarch, who had gotten his start as an apprentice pork butcher at age thirteen, for remaining down-to-earth even after becoming head of the company. Between meetings, for example, Auguste liked to pop into the cutting room, an eight-inch knife in hand, and carve up a few carcasses. But the mere thought of Auguste meeting his mother's second husband, a very buttoned-down CEO of a yogurt multinational, made Mathieu cringe.

The television crew arrived at eleven o'clock, and the reporter began her interview with a predictable enough question.

"What new products will you be unveiling at this year's show?"

Auguste puffed up with pride. "After the very successful launch of our garlic cocktail sausage, we're competing for the Industry Gold Award with a new product that I think will create quite a stir: a wild-berry sausage."

Mathieu lamented not being in Auguste's place. Like the cocktail sausage, the wild-berry sausage was *his* baby. He'd had the idea upon returning home from his summer vacation and finding nothing in the kitchen but an old piece of sausage and a package of frozen blueberries. With this new product, he hoped to oust Jean-Sylvain from his place as the company's unofficial number two.

Monopolizing the microphone, Auguste was now saying that thanks to its integrated livestock operations, Nedelec Pork was one of the few firms in the sector that could guarantee full traceability for its products. Knowing how eager journalists could be for sensationalism, Mathieu foresaw an incident of some kind. The next question removed all doubt.

"What do you say to those who accuse livestock farmers of spreading swine flu, mistreating animals, and contaminating the groundwater?"

Blood rushed to the CEO's cheeks. When he spoke, his booming voice acquired a few more decibels. "First of all, who's suggesting such claptrap?"

"Environmental groups, animal welfare activists, vegetarians—"

"Vegetarians!" shouted Auguste.

"Yes, people who refuse to eat meat." The reporter looked ready to dodge a physical assault.

"I know who they are!" Auguste's face blazed fiery red. At this moment, he looked as if he would gladly have shredded this impudent hussy's stomach and intestines into ribbons, pickled them, and stuffed them into casing made from her own behind. Mathieu could see this as clearly as he could predict the old man's imminent catastrophic gaffe. And his sixth sense did not fail him.

"Listen, no carrot-munching ayatollahs are going to tell us what to do!" And he thrust a finger toward some visitors sampling meat products at his stand. "Look at these people. Are they murderers? Dangerous criminals? Do I look like a criminal to you, little lady?"

Carrot-munching ayatollahs—now he'd really done it.

Before moving to Rennes, Mathieu hadn't had any special opinion of vegetarians. At most, he'd viewed them as little green men from another galaxy with indecipherable intentions. But after seeing them on TV blocking the paths of trucks transporting hogs to slaughter here in the region of Brittany, he'd become aware of the danger they presented. Malnourished and aggressive hippies, clearly in some sort of sect, knowing no limits in their efforts to convert the world to herbivorism. But to say as much on TV—Auguste had clearly lost his marbles.

Three

At La Dame Verte, chandeliers made out of metal wheels adorned with wooden spoons lit up a dining room empty of customers but full of round tables and freshly repainted chairs. On the counter, an old cash register, restored at great expense, provided a retro touch.

Léa shivered in the cold air of the dining room. She dropped her purse on the floor, poured herself a glass of wine, and sighed. To think that she'd hoped to find a customer—at least one—dining here tonight! What an idiot she was.

She'd tried to give La Dame Verte a unique kind of décor, combining vintage and recycled items. But how ugly these placemats made from old corks were, when you really looked at them. As for the set of copper saucepans hanging from the bicycle wheels on the ceiling—where had she gotten such an absurd idea? Why hadn't she followed the lead of most vegetarian restaurants, which usually opted either for incense-perfumed Indian themes, or a horticultural look with nightmarishly large fruit and vegetable moldings?

True, her kitchen equipment would have inspired envy in a chef of a three-star restaurant, but her eyes had been bigger than her stomach. The custom-built oven, industrial bain-marie unit, and electric tilting kettle had swallowed up half of her savings by themselves. She had enough utensils and cake molds to meet the needs of a dinner rush at the fanciest Parisian restaurant. Another mistake was the costly granite work surface. Why hadn't she opted for Carrara marble from Tuscany while she was at it?

She pushed the kitchen door open and was annoyed to see a young woman in an apron sitting in a corner, a tub of potatoes at her feet. Very pale in complexion, her red hair twisted into a bun and secured with a silver, dolphin-shaped barrette, she was lost in a magazine article.

"Hi, Pervenche. What're you reading?"

"An interview with David Lynch about transcendental meditation."

"Ah." In that case, the potatoes can certainly wait, thought Léa, forcing herself not to make the remark out loud. "Aren't you going to ask me how it went in Paris?"

"You didn't even say why you were going."

"I didn't? Sorry. It was to ask for a loan."

"And?"

"And ... next time I go to a bank, it'll be to rob it." She thought back to Jean-Claude's face when, instead of smacking it, she had treated him to her usual long-winded speech on vegetarianism.

"*Annica,*" replied Pervenche. That was her favorite word. In Pali, an ancient language of India, it meant that everything is impermanent, ephemeral.

"Yes, I should keep things in perspective. After all, I could have fallen out of the TGV at a hundred and fifty miles an hour, but I didn't."

A bubbling sound and a pleasant aroma of spices

emanated from a stock pot on the stove. Léa leaned over to smell it, then fished out a ball of grayish matter and tasted it.

"Don't you think it needs a little more carob flour?"

"Listen, I've agreed to cook that stuff, but don't count on me to eat it."

You'd think I'd asked her to make rabbit fricassee or veal tenderloin, Léa thought irritably, doing her best to open her chakras. This "stuff," as Pervenche called it, was made from tofu, wheat gluten, almonds, celery, and other completely plant-based ingredients. Léa had had the idea the previous night, in one of the creative flashes that sometimes came to her when she couldn't sleep. She'd calculated that putting imitation meat like this sausage on her menu would bring in more customers. But Pervenche, of course, was against it. Honestly, Léa didn't know why she'd hired that girl. Sure, Pervenche accepted the pitifully low wages, but under her placid exterior she had real problems with authority and would drag her feet whenever Léa asked her to do the slightest thing. In the language of psychology, she was passive-aggressive—in other words, the nightmare of any business owner. As for Pervenche's dietary ideology, she was more skeptical of Léa's menu than even a regular omnivore would be. The idea of a tofu "sausage," seitan "steak," or vegetarian "kebabs" bothered her because of the reference to what she called not "meat" but "animal cadavers." Since humans had been gatherers before becoming hunters, Pervenche considered imitation meat products as unbearable dictates, an encouragement of what she saw as the "ideology of meat as a necessity."

Léa added the carob flour herself, then asked coldly, "Where's Charline?" Charline, her miniature pig, was Léa's closest friend for two hundred miles.

"She's upstairs sleeping," replied Pervenche.

"Did you give her those bottles I left in the fridge?"

"Of course," replied Pervenche, looking at her

reproachfully. "Although I don't understand how you can give her cow's milk!"

A sudden desire to drive a Hummer, smoke Cuban cigars, and add T-bone steaks to the restaurant's menu came over Léa. She couldn't resist. "If you know of a sow willing to donate some milk, let me know. Someone in your family surely has one?"

Pervenche's face turned pale. She flung off her apron and stormed out of the room. Weighed down with disappointment, fatigue, and now remorse, Léa turned off the burner and went up to her apartment above the restaurant.

Her dream had always been to live in a vintage setting, and she'd definitely gotten what she wanted. Both the furniture and the moths were antique. A smell of dank, humid wood and mildew hung about in the hallway. The floorboards tended to come unglued, and she would soon be able to admire the landscape with the window shutters closed, thanks to the growing cracks in the wall. In the office, her laptop computer sat on a trestle table, surrounded by recipes and loose sheets of paper on which she scribbled ideas for new dishes and other thoughts. The bedroom, painted blue, smelled of lavender and the bohemian life. A jogging outfit was collecting dust on a hanger behind the door, and a Jamie Oliver cookbook, *Rock'n Roll Cuisine*, lay on the nightstand. Two bookshelves—one full of novels, the other art history books—occupied part of the wall, and an abstract painting by her mother filled the space above the bed. Every time she contemplated this remarkable work of art, she felt a kind of support, an encouragement to keep on going.

She finally found Charline in the bathroom drinking water from a basin she'd placed under the leaking toilet tank. Although a member of the pig family, she was no bigger than a puppy. Léa had always had a soft spot for pigs, as she did for wolves and crows—all of them unloved, misunderstood, and unclassifiable animals. Pigs were the only non-ruminant animal with cloven hooves, and their intelligence placed them far ahead of dogs and cats and just behind chimpanzees, orangutans, and elephants. Saddled with an unfair reputation for laziness, pigs were actually able to run at nearly thirty miles per hour and swim so well that sailors used to bring them on their sea voyages, knowing that they always headed straight for land in the event of a shipwreck. Their internal organs were so similar to humans' that a sow could host a pregnant woman's embryo during a surgery. If certain religions prohibited the consumption of pork, it was not only for health reasons but because of this disturbing resemblance. And yet ...

Charline looked up at her mistress, who bent down and took her into her arms. The black creature wriggled with happiness, her long, straight tail swishing back and forth, and the tears Léa had been holding back for hours now found their release. "We'll get through this," she said, sobbing. "You'll see. I promise you we'll get through this."

Charline rose up on Léa's forearms and nuzzled her neck with a moist and comforting snout.

Four

"In the wonderful world of pork products, everything's looking rosy, and all indicators suggest things will stay this way for some time."

Now, that was the kind of news Mathieu liked to start an afternoon of work with. A photo of a pink pig floating on a cloud of the same color illustrated the article in the trade magazine. The market's revenues had grown by 1.6 percent in the last six months, and the outlook for the next half-year ...

The arrival of his secretary in the adjacent room, separated from his office by a glass wall, interrupted his reading.

He really liked Arlette. Although married to a retired post-office manager, she was a thrill-seeker. He still couldn't imagine this round-faced, sixty-something lady, whom he always saw dressed in well-tailored but outmoded jacket-and-skirt sets, hurling herself into the void from a 130-foot-high bridge with a bungee cord around her feet. Yet that was what she'd done the previous weekend. What new adventure would she tell him about today? Smoothing down her gray hair, which she styled in a sort of bouffant, she came over to his desk with a twinkle in her eye.

"Mathieu, you'll never guess what—I just had lunch at a *ve-ge-tarian* restaurant!"

"What!" This topped even last month's whitewater rafting. "You're joking, I hope."

"Nope. It's called La Dame Verte."

"Shh—not so loud," he whispered, casting a sidelong glance at the door.

"Huh?"

"Arlette, really! You know Auguste has a dartboard in his office with a picture of tofu on it, don't you? And that we're at war with those people?"

"Can't help it. Adrenaline is my weakness."

Her weakness! "You … " He waggled his finger at her. She was impossible. "And? How was it?"

"It was great."

"Now you're just messing with me."

"No, I'm serious. It was very light, too."

Mathieu, who could not say the same of the sausage he'd had for lunch, was annoyed by this. "Arlette! Those people are fanatics, a threat to French cuisine and the good life!"

"Oh, don't be so sure. It was very gourmet, as a matter of fact. Look, I noted down the names of all the dishes." She pulled a piece of paper from her pocket. "Beet carpaccio with arugula and avocado for the starter, followed by coconut tempeh curry for the main dish, and, finally, pears poached in sweet red wine for dessert."

Mathieu's stomach churned. He could easily imagine the place: a feeding trough full of carrots, cauliflower, and lettuce leaves. A row of pale, sad-looking individuals sitting alongside it, chewing in silence, occasionally washing down their cud with gulps of weak chamomile tea. Hare Krishna music would be playing in the background.

"How horrible!"

A confident female voice broke in. "What's horrible? What are you talking about?"

He jumped—he hadn't seen Astrid come in. She was now standing right next to Arlette, her generous curves hugged in all the right places by a gaudy blazer and skirt. He saw a look of entreaty in his secretary's eyes.

"Arlette was just telling me about a DVD she rented yesterday—*Night of the Living Dead*." He surprised himself with his aptitude for lying. An occupational hazard, he supposed. "You know she's a thrill-seeker, right?"

"No, I didn't." Astrid stared blankly at Arlette. "You can go now."

He felt bad seeing his secretary dismissed so coldly, but that would teach her to go around expressing sympathy with vegetarians at her workplace. As Astrid took a seat opposite him, pheromones and whiffs of a heady perfume struck his nostrils. *She applies her makeup with a trowel, and that shade of blonde is as believable as the promises of a campaigning politician*, protested Mathieu's metrosexual instincts, but his regular instincts had to admit they were titillated when she crossed and uncrossed her legs à la Sharon Stone.

They quickly covered current matters of business and then, lowering her voice, Astrid announced the big news: With the encouragement of his family, Auguste, whose heart was going from bad to worse, planned to gradually move away from running the company and appoint a general manager to replace him. Astrid didn't have the skills for the position herself, she said, but Jean-Sylvain was doing everything he could to get it. Mathieu, whose pulse had quickened, could not repress a grimace. He was much more qualified than Jean-Sylvain to manage the firm. That bonehead was truly beginning to get on his nerves.

"In any case, Jean-Sylvain is a wuss," said Astrid, showing the inside of her red lips. "We need someone with more get-up-and-go, more vision, someone with a real instinct for sales."

That sounds just like me, thought Mathieu, galvanized by the idea and sensing his reptilian brain and his analytical brain parting ways. Jean-Sylvain was a Nedelec, the son of Auguste's favorite brother and one of the company's many family shareholders. This was a decisive advantage, no matter what Astrid thought. *Either he knew nothing about female body language, or the way she flicked her hair meant she was coming on to him.* He now would have to fight to convince Auguste that he was the man for the job. After the garlic cocktail sausage and the wild-berry sausage, he needed to pull another fantastic idea out of his hat. A fluorescent sausage? *Right here, right now, he would like to find out what brand of lingerie she wore.* In veiled terms, she confirmed that he was her preferred candidate and that she would stand up for him to the members of her family. *Should he ask her to dinner to say thank you? He imagined the spicy turn of events that could follow.*

The conversation over, Astrid swung her hips over to the door, then turned back to look at him, flinging her hair over her shoulder one last time. The thumb in her belt loop did not escape Mathieu's notice. A direct invitation.

"By the way," she said, "the hog breeders' federation is planning a tour in Germany starting this Thursday. I was going to go with Daddy, but his doctor is against it. Would you happen to be free?"

Her thighs wrapped around him in a hotel room overlooking the Rhine River, with The Ride of the Valkyries *playing furiously in the background ...*

Astrid waited for his answer with a look that seemed to say, "When will you ever make a move?" Make a move? His analytical brain regained control. He may as well jump onto a live mine! In his current situation, going out with the boss's daughter was much too risky, especially since Auguste doted on his little girl. Mathieu liked her, that was for sure, but wasn't Rennes full of beautiful women who'd be happy to meet someone with his combination of good looks, intelligence, and charm? And if she wanted his body, she could just as well make him general manager first.

He checked his schedule and arranged his features into a look of disappointment.

"Oh, too bad. I have a meeting with the people at the Juste Prix purchasing office Thursday morning." In reality, the meeting was Wednesday, but she didn't suspect anything. Once he was alone again, Mathieu got up and began pacing the length of his office. General manager! It was too good to be true. His cell phone rang, interrupting his daydream.

"Hello?" Recognizing the voice of Henri, his stepfather, Mathieu frowned. His mother must have been badgering him to reserve their tickets to Rennes, he thought. Indeed, the old ball-buster was calling to propose some dates for their visit.

"Come whenever you want. I'm free every weekend," he replied.

"Well, don't you seem enthusiastic. By the way, I wanted to congratulate you on your Industry Gold Award." There was a pause. "Wild-berry sausage … quite a good idea, really."

"Thanks. It seemed an intriguing combination." He was taken off guard by the compliment—his stepfather was always boasting about his own son, an accounts auditor in the luxury sector. Mathieu didn't resist the temptation to rub it in. "The Nedelecs are thinking of me for general manager."

A vexed silence followed, broken by a haughty tone. "Don't count your chickens before they hatch."

"I said *thinking* of me."

"Hmm. You're pretty young for such a position, but then I don't have any experience with small companies."

"We're not that small. We take in a hundred million euros a year, after all." Big deal, Mathieu realized. The yogurt multinational Henri directed operated in fifty countries and made billions. Instead of preparing another counter-argument, Mathieu deflated like a flat tire. "Well, maybe you're right. I don't think I'll get the job."

"What a defeatist!"

"You just told me not to count my chickens."

As he put down the phone, he felt a pain in his side, just under his ribs. The sausage he'd had for lunch, or his stepfather? Good Lord! He despised this man almost as much as he hated peas or spinach, which was saying a lot. Under the pretext that Mathieu had gotten only fair grades in high school before beginning his business studies (and not at a prestigious school, like his own four-eyed offspring), Henri deemed him just good enough to be in middle management, and then only if he was well supervised. Since Mathieu's early childhood, this man had been telling him that he had an unstable nature, that he was weak-willed and easily influenced. Citing these reasons, he'd avoided offering him a job at his own company. Hmpf! Too bad for him. The old coot didn't know what he was losing.

The pain in Mathieu's side kicked in again. He'd had it for weeks now. Colon cancer? But he was only thirty-three, for Pete's sake! He turned on his computer and did a Google search for a gastroenterologist.

Five

Léa was always repelled by the produce sections of supermarkets, with their tomatoes grown in plastic greenhouses and eggplants cultivated from hybrid seeds—beautiful but flavorless. She took great care in choosing her raw materials and, after some searching, had finally found a place offering quality produce at a good price: Le Moulin Neuf. Every week, she drove the ten miles between Rennes and this organic produce farm to restock her kitchen with cabbage, onions, lettuce, leeks, endives, and zucchini. It didn't hurt that she felt a certain attraction to Robinson, the owner.

This morning, she spotted him kneeling over a bed of plants at the other end of the plot. His red bandana added a vivid touch to the palette of greens ranging from the yellow-green of the musk squash and the beige-green of the endives to the greenish-red of the rhubarb. A buzzing of insects rose up above the rectangles of planted plots separated by aisles. Breathing in deeply to savor the fresh fragrance of plant slurry and chlorophyll, Léa paused to contemplate some bugs making love in a bed of angelica flowers. Robinson, who still hadn't seen her, was stirring the contents of a jam jar while humming a Bob Marley song to his Swiss chard.

"Hi there!" she called out in an artificially casual tone.

Robinson turned his head. "Léa! How's it going?"

With his wide-brimmed hat, bandana, and three-day stubble, Robinson truly lived up to his name. Léa had heard that he'd gardened at several monasteries and Zen dojos before going into business for himself. An astrology enthusiast, he sowed his seeds according to the alignment of the stars and boosted the nutritional properties of his vegetables by adding medicinal plant essences to the soil with an eyedropper.

"Have you seen my chard?" he asked. "What do you think?"

"It's great."

The leaves, which had a bluish-green hue, were wide and fleshy. Small holes showed that the insects had taken their share, but they were free from chemical fertilizer.

"Chard is my favorite vegetable," said Robinson, placing the jar on the ground. "No need to uproot them. You can just pick off a few leaves at a time."

With a flower in his mouth, he would have fit in perfectly at a hippie protest in the seventies, Léa thought tenderly. He straightened up and pointed to a rectangle of earth left fallow.

"Over there, I'm going to plant Jerusalem artichokes and other heritage vegetables."

She began imagining recipes using Jerusalem artichokes. Each time she came here, it was the same: the poetry of the place had a real effect on her. Robinson pointed at a square of sunflowers bathing in the sun a few yards away.

"Look! They're playing."

"Uh … I don't see anything," she said, squinting at the flowers.

"Yes, look. The big ones are teaching the smaller ones how to turn. They learn through playing, like in the animal kingdom."

She smiled indulgently. "Isn't your imagination running away with you?"

"Not in the least. My plants sleep, wake up, reach toward the light with their leaves—exactly like animals."

"They're intelligent, you mean?"

"More than we realize. The ends of their roots have cells similar to our neurons, and they communicate with chemical signals." He adjusted the brim of his hat. "Haven't you ever wondered why many of our drugs—tobacco, coffee, opium, and marijuana, for example—are made from plants?"

She shook her head.

"Because they manipulate us to transport their seeds. Scientific studies have been done on this. They're amazing, I tell you!"

In his excitement, he knocked over the jam jar he'd placed on the ground. A thick, clay-colored liquid spilled out from it. "Rats!"

Léa came back down from her little cloud. "What's that?" she asked.

"A fantastic natural fertilizer," he answered, kneeling to scoop the substance back into the jar.

"Ah."

"Yep. Made from turkey."

"Huh?"

"Blood, bones, and feathers. I buy it in two-quart cans."

She suddenly felt as white and cold as a package of frozen leeks. "You … you're kidding, right?"

"Nope. I've already tried guano, vermicompost, and dried blood, but turkey is the real deal," he explained, focusing on his jar.

The disturbing realization that the vegetables served at La Dame Verte had grown out of slaughterhouse waste flashed into Léa's mind. But then she reflected. Wasn't the earth's soil already an enormous cemetery in which everything was continually recycled? And in any case, so-called "normal" food was so saturated with pyralenes, fungicides, insecticides, dioxins, miticides, herbicides, pesticides, arsenic, and other horrors that there was no real alternative to organic. She would just have to accept it. But between that and pardoning Robinson, there was a big step.

"So why do you mention only seaweed and nettle slurry on your website?" she asked him point-blank, once he had straightened back up.

"Oh, it's better for business."

"I would've preferred to know."

He shrugged his shoulders with an unconcerned air. "Organic fertilizer is very often animal-based. Everyone knows that."

"I didn't."

"You vegetarians—you can really be naive sometimes!"

Léa was so surprised she didn't even get angry. "What? You eat meat?"

"Of course. I eat organic, but I'm no vegetarian."

∿

Léa stewed in her disappointment all the way back home. How had she not seen that behind this gentle dreamer there hid an unscrupulous businessman and carnivore? This confirmed the distinction she had always made between organic food enthusiasts, most of them omnivores, and vegetarians. Those who championed organic cared about their health and the environment but tended to forget the issue of animal suffering. Yet organically raised livestock was slaughtered at the same age and under the same conditions as in the traditional system.

In any case, Robinson had just joined Léa's already

long list of romantic disappointments. How much simpler vegetables were! The ugliest ones were the tastiest—you couldn't go wrong. But if their flavor came from turkey blood, ugliness was no longer a decisive factor. What to do, then? How could you know when you had the right one, whether it was a question of men or leeks? But this question presupposed the existence of an ideal man, a theory that remained to be proven.

Changing perspective, she wondered whether it might not be more useful to compare representatives of the male gender to the characterless or even toxic vegetables that could be transformed into wonderful things in the right hands. Winter squashes lost their blandness when you added ginger, cloves, or nutmeg, for example. And once its fearsome prussic acid was extracted, manioc could be made into delicious savory pancakes.

Six

Always the same thing, Mathieu thought in annoyance. A half-dozen of them were trapped there again, early in the morning, listening to Auguste ramble on in this dreary meeting room. If only he could sleep through it! But the man kept punctuating his words by slamming the side of his hand down on the oval table, as if he were still hacking off pigs' feet in his grandfather's butcher shop, which was featured in a large sepia photo hanging on the wall. Mathieu contemplated it. On the threshold of the establishment was little Auguste, in a baby carriage, between two men: his father on the one side and, holding a piggy bank in his hands, his grandfather on the other. Mathieu had seen this bank before. A collector's piece made of Meissen porcelain, it sat on the CEO's desk, symbolizing the Nedelec clan's success over four generations.

Suddenly, with no warning, Auguste exploded into a rant against a celebrity culinary critic. "As if we didn't already have enough problems with the vegetarians! Now this idiot is trying to tell us how to make our sausages!"

"Daddy, your blood pressure," Astrid said.

"Leave me alone about my blood pressure!" *Wham!* "I'm proud of my blood pressure and cholesterol levels, young lady!" *Bam!*

Mathieu looked to see whether Auguste's karate chop had left a mark in the heavy oak table. Finally, things were starting to get interesting.

"These attacks on our industry are unfair, but we have no choice," broke in Jean-Sylvain, whose bargain-bin cologne was stinking up the room. "We have to try to weather the storm."

"Let ourselves be cut up into pieces, you mean?" growled Auguste.

"Pork is the most frequently consumed meat in France," his nephew continued. "Over seventy-five pounds per inhabitant per year, fifty-five of them processed products. Nothing will ever take away our countrymen's taste for sausage, potted pork, or pâté. We're like croissants, the Tour de France, or the Arc de Triomphe—we're a national institution."

"Hmm. Mathieu, what do you think?"

Mathieu took a sheet of paper from the folder in front of him. This was the chance he had been waiting for. If things went as he hoped, he would be able to block Jean-Sylvain's path to the general manager's chair and get him out of the way.

"I have here the latest statistics," Mathieu said. "Sixty percent of the French population is no longer sure what they can or should eat to be healthy. And with the H1N1 virus, which some scaremongers continue to call swine flu, the situation is only getting worse. This is why we must respond with a strong initiative that leverages both quality claiming and relation building."

"Pfft!" Jean-Sylvain sighed. "What's all this jargon?"

"This jargon, as you say, represents market share." Pow! Right where it hurts! Mathieu smirked to himself. Learn the words of the trade if you want to become general manager, meathead! "With quality claiming, we adopt a circumvention strategy, highlighting a healthful ingredient in our offering—for example, the berries in our wild-berry sausage. With relation building, we shift the dialogue with our customers to something that helps create affinity and rapport."

"Aha! The best offense is defense, right?" said Auguste.

"That's what I say, too, but in normal language," complained Jean-Sylvain.

"Except that I'm talking about a proactive defense, not a passive one." Mathieu remembered a line from a presentation he'd given in his first year of business school; it had focused on export sales of almond candies from southern France. "We must prove to consumers that taste is in our genes and that we care about quality."

It was working! Auguste was salivating like an elderly basset hound.

"Well, Mathieu, if you've got an idea, spit it out!"

This was the critical moment. Astrid was already in on the plan, but Jean-Sylvain might make an attack.

"My idea is to open a museum devoted to pork products. Right here in Rennes."

"Like the Louvre, you mean?"

"Well, not exactly." Was Auguste getting a bit loopy? Did he seriously imagine Nedelec sausages in the same league as the *Mona Lisa*? "It would be more like a space of one thousand to thirteen hundred square feet with a stand where visitors can sample and buy our products, as well as a permanent display dedicated to our production methods and the nutritional benefits of our offerings."

"Hmm." Auguste rubbed his nose. "You're serious about this?"

"It's the result of a thorough strategic analysis."

Astrid gave him a look of support, and Jean-Sylvain tapped on his calculator in a frenzy.

"TV advertising isn't as effective as it used to be,"

Mathieu continued. "The Internet is saturated and not well suited to products such as ours. We need to focus our efforts on point-of-sale advertising, but in terms of image, the benefits are pretty small. This museum would give us credibility and exposure while bringing us closer to the consumer. I've done some benchmarking of our competitors, and they're all doing things like this."

"And I've done my calculations," interrupted Jean-Sylvain, out of breath. "A place like that in downtown Rennes would cost us two or three mil."

"Financial directors!" grumbled Auguste. "Always exaggerating the costs and minimizing the benefits!"

"With all due respect, this is something for multinationals," countered Jean-Sylvain.

The head of the Nedelec clan thrust his chin toward the large sepia photograph. "I have always acted on instinct, sir! Even in my tiny fifty-square-foot butcher shop, I acted on instinct, and now my instinct is telling me that this pork museum would be very interesting to our main target—housewives under the age of fifty!"

"And I imagine it would be self-financing to some extent, with the product sales, right?" Astrid said innocently. Mathieu knew that the project truly interested her; she already had some frightening ideas for the interior.

"So we just need to find the right location, then." Mathieu smiled. "With a parking lot, of course."

Mathieu was on cloud nine. Of course, this museum was somewhat of a gamble, but at a time when the general manager position was at stake, he had proven his spirit of initiative and, most important, revealed Jean-Sylvain's lack of vision. He watched with satisfaction as Jean-Sylvain, soundly beaten, got up and left the room without another word. It was one of those jubilant moments that was enough to justify an entire career.

Seven

"So, what do you think? Léa?"

Léa jumped like the class dunce caught daydreaming by her teacher. "Uh … sounds good to me," she said.

"So, we'll count you in."

When she realized the conversation had been about handing out free veggie burgers at a shopping center, she regretted her answer, but she'd been distracted by her current problems. She was at Le Chat Qui Fume, an old café downtown where the Rennes Vegetarian Society met once per month. What had prompted an individualist such as her to join this organization? True, its members represented half of her meager clientele. But that wasn't all. For an idea to gain ground, you need to share it, even if you don't have that much in common with everyone else.

Léa glanced around at the people sitting nearest her. Lorelei, a former model, not only followed a vegan diet but also refused to wear any clothing made from wool or silk, or to use any beauty product that had been tested on animals. The chic of the chic. As for Jean-Christophe and Marie-Chantal, they had converted to vegetarianism after a miraculous food-poisoning episode in Lourdes. And then there was Max, who dreamed of imposing a new herbivorous world order and dragging all the meat producers before the International Criminal Court of The Hague.

"That's a waste of time! It's better to block the pig trucks," Max complained.

He was wearing a T-shirt that read MEAT IS STILL MURDER. He probably listens to The Smiths on a loop, thought Léa, who was dismayed by his ideas. A debate was arising between the diehards and the moderates of the organization. Léa herself leaned more toward the moderate point of view. She did not agree with John Harvey Kellogg, a pioneer of the vegetarian movement, who seemed to consider that eating a steak was tantamount to suicide. Neither did she see meat-eaters as criminals; her grandfather sliced up a rack of lamb every Sunday, but he wouldn't hurt a fly! No—if there were any culprits, they were the meat producers who encouraged overconsumption of their products while concealing the negative effects on human health and the environment. But shocking people by covering yourself in fake blood and lying nude in a gigantic, plastic-foam meat tray in downtown Rennes—one of the favorite pastimes of Max and his friends—was not the right way to fight this fight. Max now suggested filming the living conditions of pigs at a hog farm and putting the videos on YouTube.

"You know that's illegal," said Norbert, the organization's president. "Blocking those trucks that other time brought us nothing but trouble."

Norbert was seventy-five years old, a small, wiry man with medium-length gray hair, his alert, nervous face adorned with wobbly glasses. As the discussion became more heated, Léa slipped away. She had no time for Max's extremist lunacies. They were supposed to be discussing plans for Veggie Pride, which would be taking place in one week. Plus, she was eager to taste the eggplant-and-Brazil-nut terrine she had put into the oven with a preprogrammed bake time. As with each new recipe she invented, she was torn between the fear of failure and the hope of a great new discovery.

A voice called out to her as she made her way to her car under the night sky. "Hey, Léa … "

She turned to see Julien, a prominent gastroenterologist, standing a little way behind her. He was separated from his wife and had a twelve-year-old daughter, Susie, who was also a member of the organization. He looked a bit nervous. "When I saw you leaving, I decided to go as well," he explained apologetically. "Actually, I have something I wanted to tell you."

"Uh … I didn't see Susie with you tonight." Léa stalled, noticing with alarm that they were alone in the street. "How is she?"

"She's well, thank you. She's at her mother's place. There's no school this week."

"Ah, yes, school vacation!" What was wrong with her? Her voice trembled and her hands were clammy. "You were saying?"

"It's a little difficult," he began, as if he were announcing to a patient barely out of the operating room that he'd accidentally left a scalpel in her intestines. "I … uh … I hope you won't take this the wrong way or think badly of me, but I … "

"Yes?"

"Well, I … "

"I'm sorry, but it's late, and I have to get up early," she said hurriedly. Men! It was exactly what she'd been afraid of: He was going to ask her out! Of course, he wasn't the ugliest or least appealing guy in the world, but he couldn't have chosen a worse moment. She turned to go.

"No, Léa, wait! It's just … I ate some foie gras."

"Foie gras? You mean duck liver?"

"I know, it's horrible."

"Not at all!" What a relief! She couldn't see herself—*really* couldn't see herself—with a guy in his forties who had a twelve-year-old kid.

"You can't imagine how good it is to hear that!" said Julien. "If Susie found out, she'd go live with her mother. She calls me every day to ask how her ducklings are doing. For her, ducks are like the sacred cow of the Hindus."

"Well, it's not such a big deal. We all have our little moments of weakness."

"We're talking about an entire block of foie gras!"

"Oh, well. The quantity hardly matters." A whole block! It was, in fact, revolting, but she didn't want to drive him to suicide.

"That texture, that slightly metallic aroma, the way it melts in your mouth!" His eyes glistened. "Can you tell me the name of a vegetarian foie gras, or something similar?"

How could she have attributed libidinous intentions to such a scrupulous and polite man? She must have a serious emotional deficiency. Full of remorse, she tried to redeem herself. "There's a veggie version out there, but it's not the best. Give me a few days, and I'll come up with a recipe of my own."

"You would do that? That's great! I'm really afraid of another relapse. Especially with the two bottles of Sauternes still in my wine cellar."

"It's normal to give in to your weaknesses at the beginning. In my case, in the early days, my brain would sometimes disconnect, and I would find myself with a chicken tandoori or turkey breast on my plate. The hours I spent beating myself up about it afterward! By the way, did you go veg because of Susie?"

"As a doctor, I was already convinced of the health

benefits, but it was mainly because of her, yes. She will no longer eat anything with eyes. But it's certainly not easy. Before, I could cook a chicken breast or a steak in a few minutes, but now ... " He threw up his arms. "Vegetarian cooking takes so long!"

"It doesn't have to. There are tons of very easy recipes."

"Like what?"

"Blanquette of seitan, tofu with peanuts and mustard sauce ... "

"Mmm. I'm sure those are good, but I'm hopeless in the kitchen. And you can't get ready-made vegetarian meals at the store." That was, in fact, a major oversight of the food industry in France.

Léa gave him her nicest smile. "If you'd like, you can stop by the restaurant sometime, and I'll give you an intensive course in vegetarian cuisine."

"Oh, I'd love to, but ... I have too much work."

～

Back at La Dame Verte, she went straight to the restroom to look at herself in the mirror. Had she lost all of her appeal? That was what Julien's refusal of her invitation seemed to suggest. Although she'd made the offer purely in the spirit of solidarity, his obvious effort to keep a distance felt like a slap in the face.

She dragged herself to the kitchen and took the eggplant terrine, still warm, from the oven. In the silence of the room, she brought a forkful to her mouth. Her taste buds' verdict was irrefutable. It was like a failed attempt by a first-year culinary school student. The chopped thyme and cilantro added no flavor at all, and pine nuts would have been much better than Brazil nuts.

Léa flopped into a chair. Had she lost her touch? What had happened to the lightness she'd achieved with her grilled vegetable terrine with arugula pesto and grilled almonds? As she reflected, she realized that it wasn't a technical problem. She liked cooking because it was a humble, ephemeral art in which your ego didn't get in the way. Composing a sublime symphony, writing a book, making a film, or painting a work of art was not incompatible with a hatred of the human race; making a successful eggplant dish, on the other hand, was. Hadn't she just taken Julien, that nice family man, for a skirt-chaser? And why had she been so horrible to Pervenche? It occurred to her that her solitude and the difficulties of the moment were starting to make her irritable and misanthropic. For a cook, that was worse than losing a finger would be for a pianist. She was beginning to lose her taste for human company, which was the same as losing her taste, period. Fighting back her tears, she threw the terrine into the trash.

Eight

Sitting at his desk, Mathieu pulled a cured sausage out of its wrapper, cut off a slice with his pocket knife, and tasted it cautiously. Exactly as he'd thought. It had no flavor and should have been sold not at a supermarket but in a pharmacy, by prescription only. Yet this eight-percent-fat sausage had won the gold medal at the agricultural trade fair. The least fattening, the lowest amount of salt, the least this or the least that was the latest trend on the market. The French wanted to continue stuffing themselves with pork products, but without the risk of arteriosclerosis, diabetes, or high blood pressure. Even the *Pork Industry Code of Practice*, which lay on the corner of his desk, predicted a 10 percent reduction in the amount of salt and fat used in the industry in four years' time!

He started at the sound of a door opening. A bit ill at ease, he saw Astrid enter Arlette's office, a smile on her lips. Since they'd begun collaborating on the pork museum project, her skirts had been growing shorter and shorter before his eyes, and he and Astrid had begun speaking more familiarly to each other.

She sat down across from him. "What's this, eating sausage in secret?"

"No, I'm benchmarking." He cut a slice for her. She popped it into her mouth eagerly but immediately made a face.

"Yuck! What's this?"

"A low-fat sausage."

"You really think this can help people lose weight?" she asked, unconvinced. "Whatever you do, don't show it to Daddy!"

"Did you know that over a hundred million euros' worth of low-fat sausages were sold last year?"

"Maybe so, but that will never fly with Daddy."

Daddy, Daddy, Daddy! He was so tired of hearing that. Did she also yell out "Daddy!" when she had an orgasm? It was Mathieu's job to remember that taste, the "pleasure factor" in their jargon, was indispensable. But regardless of what the Nedelecs thought, consumer concerns such as weight loss and health were gaining ground. Sooner or later, they would have to get on board and play the health card. And from experience, he suspected that Astrid was right—Auguste wouldn't be open to this innovative approach. The boss's motto was "pork never makes you fat if you eat it in moderation." Furthermore, he hated having his habits disrupted. A former R&D manager had found himself in the Rennes unemployment office merely for daring to warn Auguste of the allergens and ionized elements in his products, Mathieu recalled. He wrapped the sausage back up and smiled at Astrid.

"What brings you here?"

"The real estate agency called. This time, they're sure they have what we need."

"Great!" he replied, in a slightly forced tone.

"They say they can show it to us today, but I can't make it. Would you mind going to have a look?"

"Well, I would have preferred to go with you, but I can

scout it out. We'll go together another time."

Like a pair of turtledoves looking for a love nest, he thought. But what they were looking for was a site for their pork museum. Against all expectations, this initiative, intended above all to eclipse Jean-Sylvain, had stirred up some senile dreams of grandiosity in Auguste—dreams that his daughter shared enthusiastically. Mathieu tried again to curb her enthusiasm.

"We could start with a simple showroom ... "

"No way. Daddy wants to attract foreign tourists. Why, are you having second thoughts?"

"No, of course not." Actually, he was. This museum was a colossal expense with uncertain profitability. If it didn't work out, Jean-Sylvain would gleefully carve him up with a bone saw.

Arlette came in to remind Mathieu of his appointment with a manufacturer of promotional stuffed animals.

A look of displeasure settled on Astrid's face. "Really, Arlette! Can't you see that we're in the middle of a discussion?"

"Uh ... yes, of course."

"Am I invisible or something?"

Later, after Astrid had gone, Mathieu called his secretary back in.

"I'm sorry about the way Astrid treated you. She can be a bit abrupt sometimes," he said.

"Oh, it's no big deal."

"Ah, okay then."

Arlette touched her forehead. "Come to think of it, I wonder why she insisted that I be assigned to you."

"She did? I had no idea."

"Yes. It would have been so easy to find a young girl for the job ... someone more energetic and efficient."

"Perhaps she's a bit jealous?" It was a trait he'd already noticed in Astrid—jealousy and possessiveness. He would be wise to watch his back.

Arlette placed a thoughtful finger on her lips. "Hmm. Hadn't thought of that." In female language, that meant she agreed.

"In any case, I wouldn't give you up for all the tea in China," he assured her. It was true. Arlette was the only person in the company with whom he didn't feel obliged to wear the Super Effective Marketing Director mask all the time. And although she looked like Mrs. Butterworth, she had a subversive side to her that he liked, at least in small doses. He was on board with the company spirit, but there was more to life than presliced ham and snack-pack sausages.

∽

The site Astrid had told him about was a rare pearl. It wasn't right in the middle of downtown, but it was only a short walk from Esplanade Charles de Gaulle, one of the city's main areas of activity. It had good road access and was big enough for a large building and a parking lot. The only problem, Mathieu noticed, was the old structure flanked by a small yard at one end of the plot. The real estate agent explained that it was a vegetarian restaurant.

"Vegetarian?" Mathieu shuddered. Auguste was going to have an aneurism. "It wouldn't be La Dame Verte, by any chance?"

"That's the one."

Arlette's new favorite restaurant, on top of it all!

The agent explained that La Dame Verte had been founded by a chef from Paris named Léa Rystel. But customers were not exactly lining up at the door. It was only a matter of weeks, or even days, before her bankruptcy papers would be filed.

Mathieu could not hide his satisfaction at hearing

this. He tried to imagine Léa Rystel—yet another of those existential-angst-searching-for-the-meaning-of-life-postmodern hippies! He would take great pleasure in personally booting her out of Rennes. But what if the real estate agency was overly optimistic about this impending closure? It was lunchtime, so he decided to find out for sure.

As he approached La Dame Verte, he removed his tie and ran his fingers through his hair to tousle it. Given their poor diet, these vegetarians surely weren't so dangerous, but you couldn't be too careful. Best to pass incognito. Trying to look casual, he scoped out the front of the restaurant. The rickety-looking windows and chipping paint conveyed a sense of failure and abandonment that the potted geraniums could not hide. Yet the restaurant was full, he noted as he approached the open door. Had the real estate guy made a mistake? In a way, the fate of his pork museum depended on the answer to this question. Driven forward by a sense of duty, he fell into step with a group of customers entering the dining room.

How noisy it was! He'd always imagined that vegetarians ate in silence, but this group was making quite a racket. Truth be told, these people seemed remarkably normal. When an old lady eating a plate of colorful food smiled at him, he was almost disappointed not to see any green bits stuck between her teeth. The restaurant didn't smell like rancid cabbage, nobody was wearing a tunic woven out of hemp, and the walls were not decorated with symbols from any of those Asian export religions, which he had always seen as unfair religious competition. A group of men engaged in a lively conversation, with a wine bottle on their table, threw him completely. So, these creatures enjoyed their food, laughed, and even drank alcohol!

But he was most amazed when a tiny red-haired woman, her bun held in place with a dolphin barrette, appeared from the kitchen holding a plate of sausages in each hand.

Speechless, he pointed at the plates. "Uh ... this is a vegetarian restaurant, isn't it?"

"Oh, these! Don't worry, these sausages are meat-free."

"Ah, that's a relief!"

"I know. I told Léa it could disturb our more sensitive customers, but did she listen?" The woman rolled her eyes.

It was true—he *was* sensitive, and the idea of a meatless sausage depressed the hell out of him. But it was too late to turn back. "Any tables left?"

She directed him to the only free table, at the back near the swinging kitchen doors. Determined to make the best of it, he took a seat and looked over the menu. Szechuan tofu, coconut tempeh curry, sliced seitan, and portobello gyoza? It was all Greek to him. Come to think of it, he would have liked to try the sausage, but he wasn't sure the waitress would approve, and he was hoping to get some information out of her.

To be on the safe side, Mathieu ordered pumpkin wonton soup as a starter, mushroom and polenta mousseline as his main dish, and flourless chocolate cake for dessert. He kept his menu to study while he waited. He noticed that certain dishes were labeled *vegan*—containing neither dairy nor eggs, according to the fine print at the bottom of the page—and figured that vegetarians must accept these two sources of animal protein in their diet. What a bunch of hypocrites! Where were animal rights in that equation? Vegans were at least consistent. Although if you looked closely enough, you would probably find larvae, termites, and other insects in a sack of grain. No, it was virtually fraudulent, just like these recycled-fiber napkins and those salt-and-pepper shakers made from old light bulbs. Ever since a girlfriend had dumped him because he had "the carbon footprint of a midsize airplane," he had hated anything and everything to do with the environment.

The interminable wait for his food gave him ample time to check out the other diners in the crowded room. These slackers clearly weren't in a hurry to get anywhere. Some had finished eating, but they all stayed where they were, chatting animatedly. He heard the word "demonstration" two or three times and became more uncomfortable. He saw the little waitress coming out of the kitchen for the umpteenth time and called her over. She was out of breath and appeared overwhelmed.

"Tell me, do you always have this many customers?"

"*Annica.*"

And she was gone. *Annica*? Was he supposed to know what that meant? He hadn't majored in Asian languages, after all. He waited for her to come back with his soup and tried another tactic.

"Business is great, huh?"

"Tell me about it. It's exhausting!" she replied with a grimace. "I didn't get to meditate this morning, and I have a bad sankhara that's hurting my back."

"Uh … of course." Good grief! This girl seemed to have overdosed on magic mushrooms. He wouldn't learn anything from her.

Spoon in hand, he contemplated his pumpkin wonton soup apprehensively, as a cat might look at a puddle of water blocking its path. But he was starving, so he brought a spoonful of the concoction to his mouth. He could always spit it out if it was too disgusting. But the wontons had a nice texture, the pumpkin was smooth and savory, and the broth offered a tasty combination of ginger and garlic. It actually wasn't bad at all. When the main course arrived, he attacked it with less apprehension. Mushrooms and polenta—they went together well enough, he figured. Apart from the polenta, which was a bit too much like solidified couscous without the customary merguez sausage, it was quite edible. Then dessert—chocolate was a universal language, he mused, spoken on both sides of the dietary border.

Congratulating himself for his bravery, Mathieu took stock of his first vegetarian meal. On the whole, it was okay. Nothing to go bananas over, as Arlette had, but also nothing like the tasteless gruel he had expected. Yet, as surprising and exotic as it was, this food didn't stick to your ribs. Where was the full-belly feeling you got from a nice plate of veal roulades or sautéed kidneys, for example?

As he was finishing his organic coffee, a young woman wearing a floppy red chef's hat emerged from the kitchen a few steps away. Could this be Léa Rystel? After the shrew he had imagined, counting her fleas next to a cauldron of nettle soup, the contrast was striking. Green eyes, narrow face, a button nose ... she was not without her charm. About his age, he figured. But she wasn't his type. He liked voluptuous, buxom women, and she was slender. A few locks of blondish hair had slipped out from under her hat. She rubbed her hands on her white apron and contemplated the dining room with an indecisive and emotional expression. He became irritated when he caught sight of a tear running down her cheek. Given his plans to eradicate La Dame Verte, he would have liked an adversary made of stronger stuff.

"Are you Léa Rystel?" he asked.

She nodded, wiping the tear on a corner of her apron. He crossed his feet under the table as if preparing for a difficult sales negotiation. "I wanted to compliment you on your menu," he continued. "That polenta and mushroom mousseline was superb!"

"Oh! I just try to show people that vegetarian cuisine isn't bland or boring."

"You're preaching to the choir over here." He smiled, then searched for an uncompromising expression. "I'm a supporter of vegetarism."

"Vegetarianism, you mean?"

"Yes, vegetarianism, of course." Damn it! At this rate, he

was going to end up in the organic garden compost behind the restaurant. "Tell me, is it better to make a reservation for my next visit?"

"A reservation!" The young woman's eyes lit up, but the spark immediately faded. "Oh, no. Today is a special case."

"Ah."

She gestured toward the dining room. "These people have come from all over western France for the organizational meeting for Veggie Pride, which is taking place this Sunday."

Veggie Pride—what absurdity was that?

Léa took off her hat and wedged it under her arm. He couldn't help admiring her hair—a natural blonde, he noted with interest—as she added, "If you live here in Rennes, try to come."

"I'll be there." Yeah, right! If this Betty Guerilla Crocker was looking for volunteers to burn trucks or blow up slaughterhouses, she shouldn't hold her breath. "Tell me, that bratwurst, what's it made of exactly?"

"Why, does it bother you that it looks like meat?"

"On the contrary."

"Oh! You aren't vegetarian?"

What kind of question was that? He didn't have fangs or claws, after all—he was almost insulted. But he played along. "No, no, I am vegetarian, of course. It's just that I'm open to innovation and have nothing against meat substitutes."

She seemed to relax. She explained the recipe, which left him speechless. A sausage that not only contained no meat, but also had no MSG, gelling agents, color additives, stabilizers, or polyphosphates? It was unnatural!

"I've already made a ham with a fake rind, and right now I'm working on a vegetarian foie gras," she added with a hint of pride.

He gulped. "For real?"

"It's for a friend who's addicted and wants to detox."

She was the one who needed to detox. He thought for a moment. "Kind of like methadone, then?"

"You could say that. At the beginning, I was rather opposed to meat substitutes myself, but if they can help bring carnivores over to our side, why not? After all, it's the best proof that we can easily do without meat."

Do without meat! He felt himself rebelling with every fiber of his being. And why not do without hot water and aspirin, too, while she was at it? Perhaps Auguste wasn't being so paranoid about the vegetarian threat after all.

Léa went back to the kitchen. As he asked the waitress for his check, Mathieu realized he was still hungry. What a rip-off! He would never make it to dinnertime without a ham-and-butter or pâté-and-pickle sandwich.

Still, he wouldn't have minded chatting a while longer with that eccentric chef. Even though she wasn't his type— and he surely wasn't hers—she was the first vegetarian he'd ever met. It was like encountering an alien. Except there was no visible deformity—green skin, antennae sprouting from her head, crooked little finger—to indicate that she was any different from normal people. Logically, therefore, the problem with these people, or their deformity rather, was something internal. An invisible attribute that made them all the more dangerous.

Nine

As soon as Léa took one hand off Charline to rummage through her purse for a tissue, the pig seized the opportunity to make a break for it. Pervenche, who was standing next to Léa, tried to grab her but got tripped up by her cumbersome rabbit costume. Léa set off in pursuit of Charline, stepping over her employee, who lay on the ground wincing in pain, the ears of her costume flopping down over her eyes. A commotion was arising in the crowd of several hundred people who had assembled in the city hall plaza to celebrate Veggie Pride. A young woman tried to block the fugitive's path with a sign, but the little feet and swinging feather-duster tail quickly changed course and headed off in another direction.

Having lost sight of Charline, Léa began panicking and slammed straight into a man with a megaphone in his hand. She stammered a few apologies, then grabbed the megaphone.

"Léa Rystel here. My pet pig has just run away. A free meal at La Dame Verte for whoever finds her!"

Perhaps her reaction was a bit excessive, but the laughter that rippled through the crowd really hurt. Between the owner of her building, who was demanding several months of unpaid rent, and the phone calls from the credit institution for the kitchen equipment, she'd had a nightmarish week. All she needed now was for an accident to befall Charline.

To her great relief, Susie, Julien's daughter, appeared a few seconds later with the runaway in her arms. Squeezed into a yellow chick costume, the girl was accompanied by a man in a horse mask. Léa kissed Charline and gave Susie a grateful smile.

"Thank you. You've just won a free meal at La Dame Verte."

"Oh, it was nothing. She ran straight into my legs." Susie petted Charline. "Hey, Dad, can I get one, too?"

Julien lifted up his mask. "We already have a dog, two hamsters, and three ducklings," he protested halfheartedly. "Don't you think that's enough?"

He pulled the mask back down. The doctor had been dragged here by his daughter and didn't want to be recognized, Léa guessed. Demonstrators like the ones at this event, whose fangs seemed to grow along with their dedication to the cause, made her uncomfortable, too. What was the point of all these slaughterhouse scenes; these photos of dead ducks, cows, and chickens; this abundance of red and black and the words *murder* and *murderer* repeated ad nauseam on all the signs? Trying to promote vegetarianism by focusing on animals and their suffering was a mistake. It worked only with people who really loved animals and alienated the rest, the majority, for whom human health, environmental protection, world hunger, and culinary innovation were much more effective arguments. When would vegetarians realize that people, and especially the French, think with their stomachs—that it's their weakness? Only Léa's friendship with Norbert, the president of the organization, prevented her from hightailing it.

The first slogan to ring out from a megaphone confirmed

her fears. "We are all a-ni-mals!" Several people joined in enthusiastically: "*We are all a-ni-mals!*"

What an idea! Of course we're all animals, but saying it too loudly wouldn't win them any friends among the non-human denizens of Noah's Ark. Suddenly, Léa noticed a head of fiery red hair bobbing through the crowd. Pervenche was heading her way, followed by a reporter and a cameraman.

"There she is!" shouted Pervenche when she saw Léa.

The reporter extended his microphone, and Charline made a statement. *Snort, oiiiiink, snort, snort ...*

The man smiled. "Ms. Rystel, would you mind telling us a little about vegetarian cuisine?"

Léa reflected for a moment. In general, she didn't have a very good opinion of the media and thought even less highly of television, which she saw as a glass pacifier. But if she had the chance to talk about La Dame Verte, why not? In these difficult times, a little free publicity couldn't hurt.

The interview began. "First of all, Ms. Rystel, why vegetarianism?"

"And why omnivorism? Humans are adaptivores—they can eat almost anything, which means we have a choice. Vegetarianism is a choice."

"As the operator of a vegetarian restaurant, do you have any specific demands?"

"Yes. The right to have meat-free meals in institutional food services, for example—at cafeterias in hospitals, schools, and businesses. I'm also pretty tired of people smirking each time I say I don't eat meat."

"Some vegetarians seem as zealous as religious evangelists. Is your goal to convert the whole world by force?" asked the reporter.

"Certainly not! We try to spread information, but people have to make their own choices. One of the most important things to know is that plant-based cuisine can be just as delicious as traditional food. This is why, at La Dame Verte, we advocate a gourmet approach to vegetarianism."

"Are you serious? Do you think meatless food can stand up to a comparison with traditional cuisine?"

"Come and taste the one-hundred-percent vegetarian bratwurst at La Dame Verte, and you'll see that it's much better than the sausages made by the region's meat producers, who use collagen casings, by the way. And much healthier. Right, Charline?"

Snort, oiiiiink, snort, snort.

Satisfied, the reporter nodded at his cameraman. As for Léa, she was glad to have mentioned the name of her restaurant twice in the space of a few seconds. She felt as though she had a knife at her throat—bringing in new customers was a question of life or death.

Ten

Mathieu was strolling down a pedestrian street crowded with people when he noticed something strange. No, he wasn't dreaming—it was indeed a shower stall with two young women in it, soaping each other with smiles on their faces. He joined the gawkers, and what he read on the shower wall chilled his blood just as much as the bare shoulders of these eco-friendly nymphs had begun to warm it: It took 900 gallons of water to produce one pound of meat, according to the Food and Agriculture Organization of the United Nations. And why not 13,000 gallons, while they were at it, or an entire Olympic swimming pool? Mathieu didn't believe in these types of calculations, especially when they were done by a bunch of lazy and corrupt civil servants. What a world! You could no longer blast the air-conditioning in your car or let the hot water run while you did the dishes without feeling that you were leaving carbon footprints all over the scene of a crime.

Farther on, he saw another crowd. Another stunt by these bigoted anti-carnivores? Yep! Splashed with fake blood, two guys lay curled under plastic wrap in giant foam trays, as motionless as cutlets on the shelves of a supermarket refrigerator case. A man next to them held a sign reading 55 BILLION ANIMALS ARE SLAUGHTERED EACH YEAR WORLDWIDE, 1 BILLION OF THEM IN FRANCE. The sight was so disturbing that a little boy burst into tears. His father complained, and the man with the sign replied in an insulting tone that it was to make people think. What, among cannibals? If this diplodocus wasn't two heads taller and a hundred pounds heavier than Mathieu, he would have shown him exactly what he thought.

Now, more chanting was coming from Rue du Chapitre. "Polluting the land, polluting the water, profiting off of animal slaughter!" and "Where's your compassion? No blood for fashion!" This must be the Veggie Pride event Léa Rystel had spoken of, Mathieu realized.

As Mathieu observed the parade, the reality came home to him: There was a fire in the kitchen, and the very foundations of French cuisine were in danger. Even worse, these cursed asparagus lovers were calling for the end of the struggle between species and wanted to annihilate the entire meat sector.

What a mix of people—so many different looks and walks of life. How could such a diverse range of folks all support the same thing? A bearded professor type with glasses wore a green T-shirt reading SUPPORT YOUR RIGHT TO ARM BEARS, and two teenage girls in goth clothing held up a banner that read THE MEAT INDUSTRY SELLS MURDER.

Scanning the crowd for Léa, Mathieu joined the people following the procession. Who were they? Curious onlookers? Sympathizers? Macrobiotic diet enthusiasts? Raw foodists who didn't heat any of their food above 118 degrees Fahrenheit? Dumpster divers? Ever since Mathieu had begun learning about vegetarianism to be able to fight it more effectively, he had been surprised again and again to see how many different neuroses and mental disorders could affect the digestive system of a human being.

The procession turned into the street where the Nedelec butcher shop stood—the same one where Auguste had gotten his start. Suddenly, the two living cutlets sprinted past Mathieu, their packaging on their backs. What was going on? He would have liked to follow them, but what if he was recognized? What if there were TV crews filming the event? Not to mention that he would feel as comfortable among these fanatics as a rabbit in a fox's den. Unless he, too, could find himself a mask …

"Ne-de-lec! Mur-der-ers! Ne-de-lec! Mur-der-ers!"

Mathieu elbowed his way to the front of the procession. The idiots! It was exactly what he'd feared: Their fists in the air, a dozen frenzied activists were shouting in front of the Nedelec butcher shop. The customers took to their heels, and a string of sausages fell from an old lady's shopping bag. Sweating behind the pig mask that he'd bought off a kid in the crowd for an astronomical price, Mathieu remembered that Nedelec Pork was sponsoring the local rugby team. And the guys who played the scrum-half and prop positions worked at this very shop. All of a sudden, two young men in aprons burst out of the door. The rugby players! Their rolled-up sleeves revealed forearms the size of Bayonne hams, and with the expressions they wore, the butchers looked about as pleased as Rottweilers whose kibble has just been whisked away from under their noses.

The brawl began, and two vegetarians immediately bit the asphalt. This did not stop their companions from rushing to attack. It wasn't until one of them landed at Mathieu's feet with the thud of a watermelon that he made up his mind. Amid the shouting, he ran straight toward one of the tree-huggers with the intention of flattening him. But a straight punch to the chin sent the guy flying into his arms before he could get there. To make it clear that he hadn't tried to help him, Mathieu let him fall.

When the face of one of the butchers appeared in his field of vision, brimming with hostility, Mathieu realized his error: In his haste, he had forgotten to take off his mask. It was too late. A hand that would have made Muhammad Ali's look like a schoolboy's shoved him with such force that Mathieu lost his balance and fell down hard on his tailbone. The impact of his fall pushed his mask down over his chin.

Eleven

Police sirens wailed from a distance. Bravo, thought Léa with annoyance. With their stupid slogan chanting and penchant for violence, Max and his friends had set a match to the powder keg. It was the perfect way to confirm the fears of people who saw vegetarians as raving lunatics.

Disheartened, she was ready to go home when she noticed something strange. A man sitting on the street, rubbing his lower back … yes, it was him, the guy who had been at La Dame Verte a few days earlier and had complimented her on the polenta mousseline! She wouldn't have bet a radish that he was really a vegetarian, and yet here he was at the demonstration. She knelt down for a closer look.

"Hey there. How're you feeling?"

"It depends which part of my body you mean," he groaned, staring at Charline.

"This is my miniature pig. To tell the truth, I didn't think you'd come."

"Sorry to disappoint you."

"You should get up and make yourself scarce," she

replied, ignoring his remark.

"Why?"

"This place is teeming with cops."

"I haven't done anything wrong."

"But those others have, so you could find yourself in the paddy wagon with them."

"What?" He looked down at the pig mask hanging from his neck, then over at some nearby officers. He seemed to come back to his senses, and his eyes grew wide. "But I was only trying to … damn it!"

Léa helped him back to his feet. On a nearby side street, they came upon Julien, who was consoling a sobbing Susie. Léa introduced the two men, noticing that they seemed to size each other up suspiciously, as if sensing an instinctive rivalry. This reassured her somewhat—her appeal must not have totally disappeared.

Farther on, they ran into Norbert, who was busy reuniting his flock. His face lit up when he saw Léa and the stranger, whose hand he shook vigorously.

"Our young people have lost their heads, but I must congratulate you on what you've done."

"Uh, it was nothing. Pure reflex."

"No, it was very brave. What's your name?"

"Mathieu."

Léa noticed that Mathieu was quite uncomfortable. Too modest to take a compliment? That wasn't the impression he'd made that day at her restaurant. He seemed more like the typical Parisian executive manager who got a superiority complex as soon as he left the capital. But then again, if seedless oranges and pitless cherries could exist, why couldn't there be, somewhere in the galaxy, a guy without a monstrous ego?

"Let's go have a drink," said Norbert. "It's on me."

"Thanks, but I don't really feel up to it." Mathieu hedged.

"Oh, a little pick-me-up will do you good. I'll be disappointed if you say no. And so will Léa."

"I have to get home myself, actually," said Léa.

Norbert frowned. "Where's your vegetarian solidarity? You two aren't going to let an old man drink alone, are you?"

He ushered them into Le Chat Qui Fume, their favorite café. They sat down at a table. Léa handed Charline over to Norbert and went to the restroom. In front of the mirror, as she reapplied her fair-trade lip balm and fluffed her hair back into place, she gave herself a questioning look: *What's gotten into you? You haven't primped in front of the mirror like this for ages!* It couldn't be for Norbert, and so ... was it for this Mathieu guy? He wasn't so bad looking, true. But he had a really large nose and wore hideous checked shirts. And he'd looked at her as if she were a crazy person when she explained about Charline.

Three cognacs were sitting on the table when she got back, and Norbert, as always, was monopolizing the conversation. He had entrusted Charline to Mathieu, who seemed to be bonding with the little pig. Touched by this, Léa took her seat. Mathieu continued petting Charline with an awkward smile. They clinked glasses, and Norbert resumed his speech.

"Chimpanzees, gorillas, orangutans, and humans all share the same tooth structure, opposable thumbs, binocular vision, and intestines that are much longer than carnivores'. Why do you think this is?"

Mathieu raised his eyebrows politely.

"Well, it's because these features are adaptations to life in the trees and a fruit-based diet," replied Norbert, pushing his glasses back up.

Mathieu looked at Léa, who shrugged her shoulders helplessly; she knew by heart what was coming next.

"The absence of large canine teeth and the length of the intestines are very revealing. Our jaws are not built to kill, and our intestines are too long to digest meat without absorbing certain toxins, which in turn cause a range of diseases."

This time, Mathieu frowned. "Hmm. I'd never thought of things that way."

Léa could see that he would much rather be at home, a doughnut cushion under his bottom and a bottle of ibuprofen within reach. To be fair, Norbert was a bit eccentric. A retired paleontologist and specialist in hominid dentition, he had formerly been a follower of the so-called Paleolithic diet. This diet, based on seeds, fruit, vegetables, and barely cooked white meats, was supposed to be what hunters and gatherers had eaten forty thousand years ago. However, since grains were not allowed, it had ended up becoming a bit monotonous for Norbert, who eventually joined the ranks of lacto-ovo vegetarians. It had nothing to do with loving animals. If he loved them, it was only as skeletons or fossils excavated from geological strata.

When Norbert rose to join an acquaintance at a nearby table, Mathieu turned to Léa. "Was he serious?"

"Yes, we vegetarians are descended from apes, didn't you know that?" she replied wryly. "That said, I don't think this is the best way to convince *Homo sapiens* to give up his mammoth steak or auroch filet."

Mathieu scratched his chin. "Becoming vegetarian after studying fossilized canine teeth? You don't hear a story like that every day."

"I have an elderly aunt who is vegetarian only out of stinginess, since it's less expensive. People lump us all together, but there are as many vegetarianisms as there are vegetarians." Léa sensed that the time was right to subject him to a little questioning. "What's your field of business?"

"Information technology."

"Oh? And how did it happen for you?" She saw that he was drawing a blank. "How did you go vegetarian, I mean?"

Twelve

That was the moment when he should have admitted the truth: He worked at Nedelec Pork and was addicted to ham, sausage, and steak—in other words, they acted on his neurotransmitters and activated his reward circuits just like cocaine. She would then have returned to her Quorn, a meat substitute made with a so-called mycoprotein that these crazies extracted from a fungus, and he to his chipolatas.

So why hadn't he put an end to the misunderstanding? Was he afraid she would think he was cruel and heartless because he ate animals and enjoyed it? On this Monday morning, sitting at his desk, he was better able to assess the seriousness of his actions. Vegetarians all had a screw loose, and Léa was no exception. Hadn't she bragged about harassing a woman on the street for wearing a fur coat? And didn't she mention that she hadn't spoken to her father for years because of their differences of opinion on food? An unholy scent of chlorophyll surrounded this woman. The smartest thing would be to get as far away from her as possible, and fast—not to tell her he would visit her restaurant again soon. Wincing from the intestinal pain that had been bothering him for weeks, he asked Arlette to bring him a glass of water.

"You're so pale! Is something wrong?" she asked anxiously as she placed the glass in front of him.

"Actually, I'm worried about *you*," he replied, eyeing her bandaged right hand.

"Oh, this? It's just a scratch." The daredevil had hurt herself during an introductory cyclo-cross lesson that weekend. For a moment, Mathieu was tempted to tell her about his own misadventures. But the walls had ears—for the sake of his career, it was best to limit potential information leaks.

Arlette tidied up some things on Mathieu's desk, and then, out of the blue, began, "You know that restaurant, La Dame Verte … "

"What about it?"

"The woman who runs it was on TV."

Shoot! Did she know something? After all, they weren't in a big city like Paris. All it would take was for someone to have seen him at Le Chat Qui Fume with Léa and …

He got hold of himself. No need for paranoia. "Oh, yes! I saw that, too."

"What did you think?"

"Truly horrible," he replied, but he noticed a look of uneasiness on Arlette's face. "Don't tell me you buy into those people's propaganda? They called us murderers!"

"Maybe," said Arlette. "But she herself came across as quite moderate, and the food at her restaurant is great."

"Have you been back there?" Mathieu asked, and sighed when Arlette looked at the floor guiltily. "Arlette! I have nothing against that kind of cuisine, and I'm sure that some vegetarians are nice enough people, but given the circumstances … "

"You wouldn't shout it from the rooftops, is that it?"

He nodded, at the same time realizing that he hadn't

made such a nutritionally correct statement in a long time. In fact, what Léa had said on the news had scandalized him to the core. Promoting her fake sausage on the air, and furthermore claiming it was better than pure pork! Auguste would be in a murderous mood.

Arlette held that day's edition of *Ouest France* out to him. "Look, she's even in the newspaper."

He examined the photo. Despite her tofu-like pallor, this fanatic was undeniably photogenic. He was no longer sure that he'd lied to her because of the alcohol—it may have been for another, more nebulous, reason. In that case, it would be better not to see her again. People different from him—*complicated people*, as he called them—kindled real panic in his soul.

"Pretty, isn't she?" commented Arlette.

"Hmm ... yeah, not bad for a vegetarian."

Although, not to be mean or anything, she was as skinny as a twig. An enthusiast of the full English breakfast complete with eggs, sausage, and bacon, the curvaceous Astrid was more to his taste. As Mathieu's thoughts turned to her—she was due back that afternoon from her four-day trip to Germany with the hog breeders' federation—his intestinal pain flared up again.

∽

As soon as he entered the gastroenterologist's examination room, Mathieu's symptoms abruptly worsened. The white-jacketed doctor, a Julien somebody, was none other than that irritatingly good-looking guy Léa had introduced him to after Veggie Pride. Now, this was disturbing—the vegetarians had infiltrated all levels of society. All that was left was for them to storm the presidential palace and prime minister's office.

The doctor hesitated a moment, then smiled. "We met

yesterday, didn't we? So, what seems to be the problem?"

Mathieu described the pains he felt in his intestines and his side, just under the ribs, as well as the gas and stomach rumblings that were making his life miserable. The doctor had him lie on the examination table and palpated him in various places. Then, telling Mathieu he could put his shirt back on, he went back to his desk.

"Something been on your mind lately? Are you under any stress?"

"Why?"

"I didn't feel anything abnormal, but we shouldn't rule out irritable bowel syndrome. Nothing serious, but in some cases, stress can be an aggravating factor."

"No, no stress in particular," Mathieu mumbled.

Yeah, right. Unable to beat him in the professional sphere, Jean-Sylvain was maneuvering in the shadows to convince Nedelec Pork's smaller shareholders—his uncles, aunts, and cousins—to shoot down the company's new marketing strategy at the next shareholders' meeting. He was calling for a return to the "true pork-product tradition": tighter cost control and a shift in focus away from the large and medium-sized supermarkets and toward other distribution channels. The very opposite of what Mathieu supported.

"In any case, to be on the safe side, I'll order a test to make sure there's no blood in your stool," said Julien, taking a blank prescription sheet and beginning to fill it out.

Somewhat relieved by this diagnosis, Mathieu observed him as he wrote. A vegetarian doctor! A guy who, after nearly ten years of higher education, ended up falling into this deviant way of thinking. Was this proof that there were actually some valid scientific arguments supporting it? That would take the cake.

"Hey, doc, we vegetarians always say that our diet is healthier. But is it really true?"

Julien's pen stopped moving. "In general, yes, vegetarians are healthier than omnivores. Lower cholesterol, fewer heart attacks, less hypertension."

"So, you advise against eating meat?"

Julien colored slightly. "I'm not the best placed to moralize, but an average of two hundred pounds per inhabitant, per year, is far too much, yes."

Mathieu thought about his own consumption and made some quick calculations. "That breaks down to a half-pound per day, is that right?"

"Yes. Imagine the amount of lactic acid, saturated fatty acids, and purines you would have to eliminate from your system. Not to mention that meat is a risk factor for colon cancer and that there's a mathematical correlation between meat consumption and body mass index."

"Vegetarianism, Weight Watchers—both fighting the same battle then, if I get you right?"

"That's not what I said," corrected Julien with a smile. "But the high amount of fiber in a plant-based diet does provide a sensation of fullness that reduces your appetite for other, more calorie-dense foods."

The situation was even bleaker than he'd thought. If this charlatan could be believed, vegetarians had found a universal panacea, while carnivores were digging their graves with their teeth. But what about the much-discussed matter of animal versus plant protein? He had always heard that protein from meat was far superior to plant protein, and he posed the question to Julien.

The doctor rolled his eyes. "Ah—the myth of the better protein! How many times have I heard that? Do you know where that story comes from? A study on rats from 1914. Some researchers discovered that rats fed on animal protein grew faster than rats given plant protein. But later studies showed that although the rats grew faster, they also died sooner and had more disease than the others."

He told Mathieu that the plant kingdom also included quality protein and that by consuming both grains and legumes—semolina and chickpeas, rice and lentils, corn and red beans, for example—one could easily obtain the eight essential amino acids. "However," concluded Julien, "if someone were to go vegetarian but never eat anything but beans, they would definitely have problems."

This huckster must be getting paid by a lobby. Yet Mathieu still had a final card to play. "What about vitamin B12 deficiency? Is that a myth, too?"

"No, it's true that vegans can end up with a B12 deficiency."

"That doesn't sound good."

"It's something to watch for when you're vegan—or, in other words, a vegetarian that doesn't eat eggs or dairy products. The problem is that B12 isn't found in the plant world, or at least you can't get it in the vegetables we eat today. But it's easy to find B12 supplements." Julien held out the prescription. "Here you are. I hope I have laid your doubts to rest."

"Uh … yes."

"But don't go repeating it too widely." Julien winked. "If everyone went vegetarian, I'd be out of a job."

Vegetarian or not, Mathieu reflected, great minds think alike, for those were his thoughts exactly.

Thirteen

Auguste's office was not so big—at least, not if you compared it to a football field. A semi-trailer could easily have fit between the door and the desk. The 1970s decor, all shag carpet and orange tones, seemed to have come straight out of *The Towering Inferno*.

From the doorway, Mathieu watched irritably as Jean-Sylvain shook the CEO's hand, then sat his pompous self down with an air of ownership in one of the enormous leather armchairs facing Auguste's desk. Damn it! What was that weasel-brained moron doing here?

"Come in!" Auguste shouted to Mathieu. "You've heard about the events of this past weekend, I suppose?"

Mathieu nodded and took a seat next to Jean-Sylvain, who, as always, was sitting up straight, as stiff as a ramrod. "Blocking our trucks is no longer enough for them. Now they're attacking our butcher shops!" Auguste ranted.

He followed this with a declaration of war between the carnivore and vegetarian kingdoms that made Mathieu break out in a sweat. If the paterfamilias only knew that the vegetarians believed Mathieu to be one of their own! Mathieu jumped when the door behind him opened, but he relaxed as he saw the old man's features soften.

"My dear!" said Auguste.

Astrid, looking radiant, joined the group and happily recounted her trip to Germany. What had surprised her the most, she said, was the large amounts of processed pork products the Germans ate for breakfast.

"For breakfast!" marveled her father.

"Hold on though," said Astrid. "It's not a paradise or anything. Vegetarians are making life impossible over there, too. They already make up eight percent of the population, and they're multiplying like rabbits."

Auguste sighed. "Nothing left but to commit hara-kiri."

"I don't think we should overestimate the threat." Mathieu broke in. "Here in France, it's only two percent of the population."

"I think *under*estimating the threat they pose would be a mistake," said Jean-Sylvain with a frown. "We're dealing with fanatics—vampires who want our hemoglobin. Any member of the Nedelec family knows that."

Speaking of vampires and hemoglobin, Mathieu himself felt like going straight for this prize idiot's jugular.

"I share your opinion, Jean-Sylvain," replied Auguste. "They're bloodthirsty maniacs, but we have to respond calmly, in a dignified way." He took a rolled-up piece of paper from the table and held it out to Astrid, a gleam in his eye. "Take a look at this!"

"Oh yes, fantastic!" she cried as soon as she had unrolled the large sheet. She passed it excitedly to Mathieu, who had a hard time keeping his composure once he saw it. This horrible thing was going to be his pork museum?

Auguste's grandiloquent voice reached him as if from a great distance. "I want this museum to be a tribute to the processed-pork sector of the whole region of Brittany."

"Uh … it's sure to attract big crowds," said Mathieu cautiously. A sausage-shaped building supported by columns that looked like giant hams? "People will be curious for sure."

Jean-Sylvain examined the illustration with a disapproving expression. "It wouldn't attract big crowds unless we built it in the right place. The owner of the site we've found is willing to sell, but she still has a lease with Léa Rystel, the woman who runs that restaurant La Dame Verte."

Bam! Everyone froze as Auguste's fist slammed down on the table. His voice filled the room, the floor, the entire building. "That bitch who dared to say on television that we use artificial collagen casings?"

"Daddy, don't get upset! It's bad for your heart."

"Don't get upset? While for years now we've been using nothing but natural casings?" He clenched an enormous hand. "I'm going to sue her for slander! Run her out of business!"

Jean-Sylvain cleared his throat. "I suggest we look for another location."

Astrid fidgeted in her chair. "No, *this* is the site we need."

"Her restaurant is a bastion of vegetarianism. We would never get them out of there," argued her cousin.

Auguste raised himself up, and Mathieu shivered. The old man might have creaky joints and a few bats in his belfry, but he could still inspire fear. He pointed his index finger and directed it—thank God—at Jean-Sylvain. "*I want that site!*"

"But I swear to you, Auguste, I've tried everything," Jean-Sylvain replied. "We've reached an impasse."

An impasse? When everyone, apart from Auguste, knew perfectly well that Jean-Sylvain hadn't done a thing to try to get the site? That's the problem with inexperienced managers, Mathieu thought smugly. Sooner or later, they trip over their own umbilical cords. All he had to do now was get rid of this amateur, and Léa had given him the perfect weapon for that.

"There may be something … " Mathieu began, but suddenly, noticing that the porcelain piggy bank on the desk bore a striking resemblance to Charline, the mascot of La Dame Verte, his scruples got the best of him. For once, he doubted he could live with the ethical consequences of his actions. "No, maybe it isn't such a good idea after all."

"Are you sure?" Auguste said, looking disappointed.

"Yes, sorry."

"All right. Let's take a few days to think this over. But one thing is clear—from here on out, it's an eye for an eye, a tooth for a tooth, a sprout for a sprout." He stared at Mathieu, then at Jean-Sylvain. "I'm counting on both of you to run your gray matter overtime."

As he was about to leave the room with Astrid, Mathieu felt a heavy hand descend upon his shoulder.

"Do you have a minute?"

"Yes, sir."

The door closed.

"Have you seen the latest sales figures for our wild-berry sausages? They're selling like hotcakes! I must congratulate you again."

"Thank you, sir."

"No need for 'sir' with me. Call me Auguste."

"Yes, sir."

"You know what I think? We, the family businesses, the small companies, are the ones that'll save capitalism. The stock exchange, the CAC 40 index—poppycock! I prefer a family forum to a shareholders' quorum."

Mathieu wasn't sure he'd heard him right. He began playing with his tie.

Auguste smiled. "Blood is thicker than water. You follow? But that doesn't mean I believe in nepotism. Jean-Sylvain is good at administrative things, but he's as talented at selling ham and sausage as I am at dancing the paso doble."

Mathieu tried to maintain a neutral expression. He wasn't going to jump for joy in front of Auguste, after all.

"All doors are open to you in this company, my boy, and I do mean all," said Auguste in a fatherly tone. "The Nedelecs may be a bit hotheaded, but they aren't ungrateful. Don't disappoint me, and you won't be disappointed."

"Thank you, sir."

Was he dreaming, or had the old pimp just thrown his only daughter into Mathieu's arms? In general, bosses of family businesses paired their sons and daughters up with the children of similarly successful colleagues, so why was he talking about family to Mathieu? Why was he putting his daughter on special offer?

In any case, Mathieu was no gigolo and was not about to look for a ticket to the general manager position on the casting couch. However, if he agreed to make his contribution to the Nedelec family tree, nothing more would stand in his way at this company. Maybe he would even become CEO himself one day. Except that Jean-Sylvain would do anything to get revenge, and Astrid was the apple of Auguste's eye. The slightest misstep with her and Mr. Son-in-Law would end up in a scalding tank like an ordinary hog carcass.

"Ah! One last thing." Auguste seemed to remember. "That idea you mentioned during the meeting. I'm rather intrigued … "

Mathieu visualized himself sitting in the huge chief executive's chair a few yards away. He imagined his stepfather's shock and his mother's delight. Oh well! It was time to reap the rewards of his infiltration into the vegetarian community.

"Okay, here it is. When I went to her restaurant, I learned that this Léa Rystel had applied for a bank loan. So I wondered if we might be able to … "

"Cut off her funding, you mean? I like that idea! After all, all's fair in love and war." Auguste's hand finally left Mathieu's shoulder to retrieve a pen. "What's the name of her bank?"

When Léa had spoken of this loan after the demonstration, Mathieu hadn't been paying enough attention. "I don't know, but there's nothing stopping me from going back to find out."

"Isn't that risky? For your stomach, I mean."

"Well, I haven't noticed any serious aftereffects of that first meal, knock on wood." Deep down, he had to admit that he'd rather liked the food, but he could never say as much to Auguste, who was staring at him in horror as if they were discussing cannibalism. "It's just an unpleasant moment to get through."

"You're a risk taker, you are. Not like Jean-Sylvain. But be careful—it's a cult. It wouldn't surprise me if they do brainwashing."

"It's more the stomach-washing that scares me—at the hospital afterward."

As Auguste burst into laughter, Mathieu tried to neutralize his guilty conscience, focusing on how he would be helping reduce unemployment: Their pork museum would create a dozen jobs, while La Dame Verte, no matter what happened, was doomed to close its doors.

Fourteen

Chickpeas, caramelized onions, and raisin wine. As she contemplated the earthenware container of foie gras in the shop window, this inspiration popped into Léa's brain. Ever since Julien's confession about his withdrawal symptoms, she had been working tirelessly to create the perfect vegetarian foie gras. Coming up with a substitute that was just as good as the original had become a personal challenge for her, and she had already made several prototypes. Raisin wine! Why hadn't she thought of that before? She was sure that was the answer. Her crime against traditional French cuisine would undoubtedly earn her a lot of enemies, but who cared? If France exiled her, she would seek culinary asylum in California, where foie gras had been banned. But would she be able to reproduce that slightly metallic flavor that Julien was so fond of?

Despite her excellent memory for flavors, her last contact with foie gras was a bit hazy—it had been at a certain family party on New Year's Eve, when she'd announced that henceforth she would never eat it again. This had led to a monumental shouting match with her father, a brute devoid of the least sensitivity to the animal cause.

Léa looked up and down the street, then stole into the shop. After all, the end justified the means.

She finished the rest of her shopping and returned to La Dame Verte, where she had to sound her horn several times before Pervenche appeared, dragging her feet.

"My physical therapist told me not to do any heavy lifting because of my back," Pervenche announced as she regarded the trunk stuffed full of groceries. She bent to pick up a crate of lettuce, but Léa stopped her.

"No, take these artichokes instead, please!"

But Pervenche just stood there, continuing her complaints. "It's especially hard to do the lotus posture now."

"What do you mean? Can't you meditate in another position? In a chair, for example?"

"When will you understand that it's meditation, not relaxation?" To Léa's great relief, Pervenche finally took the artichokes and headed into the building. "Meditation doesn't work unless you suffer."

Just like with love, thought Léa, sighing as she checked that the foie gras was well hidden under the green lettuce leaves. Whew! She much preferred to bring in the crate herself. The mere thought of Pervenche's lectures if she were to discover the clandestine purchase made her shudder.

∼

Léa was standing before a large saucepan, mixing Muscat wine with star anise, cinnamon sticks, split vanilla beans, lemon juice, and a pound of sugar, when she felt the first twinges of hunger. She'd gotten up at six that morning to do her shopping and hadn't had anything but a cup of coffee. All that was left was to add a bit of Cointreau and marinate some orange and clementine segments, and she'd have a delicious spiced citrus salad for the restaurant's lunch service. She turned off the induction burner and glanced over at Pervenche, who was preparing to make a zucchini, kale, and sweet potato fricassee. After setting out the ingredients for her marinade—hoisin sauce, orange juice, shoyu, and ginger syrup—her assistant was rinsing the vegetables.

"What would you say to an omelet with Emmental cheese?" Léa asked her.

"Not for me."

"Aren't you hungry?"

"I am, but I don't eat eggs anymore. Why don't you make a vegan omelet? All you have to do is mix some chickpea flour with a little baking powder and water."

"Hmm." Léa reflected. "I'm sure that would be good, too, but I prefer eggs." Feeling a bit apprehensive, she went to the refrigerator and took out two eggs. "Have you become vegan?"

"Why? Is it grounds for dismissal?" Pervenche shot back without turning around. "You know very well that loving animals and eating eggs is incompatible. I'm just trying to be consistent."

There it was! Passive-aggressive *and* vegan. Unless she was just trying to get on her nerves? It would have been better to let it go, but Léa couldn't help herself.

"You sound just like those carnivores who try to make us feel guilty."

"If you really cared about animals, you would feel guilty on your own."

"You might recall that an egg is the unfertilized ovum of a hen, not a chick embryo."

"Yes, but the hen suffers."

"The only eggs I buy are the ones marked category zero or one. That means the hens are free-range and given the right food. There's no mistreatment in that."

"Are you sure?"

Unbelievable! As if she bought category two or three eggs, laid by hens deprived of natural light, kept confined in cages the size of a sheet of paper, and slaughtered after one year of intensive laying. That said, to answer Pervenche's question honestly … no, Léa couldn't be sure that the so-called free-range eggs were really produced under conditions that were less cruel than the industrial methods. Consumers, herself included, were so easily manipulated. But she didn't claim to be perfect. She turned the burner back on and poured some olive oil into a frying pan.

The same accusing voice rang out again behind her back. "And the cheese?"

Léa cracked the egg a bit harder than she intended, and some bits of shell fell into her mixing bowl. Was she hallucinating? Was she really having this conversation? It was usually carnivores who thought they were so smart, attacking vegetarians on this point—not members of her own camp! The egg yolks seemed to stare up at her accusingly from the bottom of the bowl.

"Did you make sure the cheese doesn't contain rennet?" asked Pervenche, coming closer. She grabbed the package of grated Emmental and turned it over.

Léa panicked.

"You didn't read the label closely enough," fussed Pervenche, making no effort to hide her satisfaction. "It's written right here: *rennet*. I'm sorry, but you're about to consume offal. Rennet is what coagulates milk protein. It's made of pieces of stomach from calves or baby goats. You know, dead ones."

Léa picked up the package and read the label. Alas, Miss Preachy was right.

"Yes, I *know* what rennet is. I just forgot to check the

ingredients," she said defensively.

"Well, next time, be more careful."

Léa could have strangled her. With an air of offended virtue, Pervenche went back to the worktable and began chopping some zucchini. *Thwack, thwack, thwack!* Although her assistant's dexterity was impressive, Léa took the opportunity to attempt to re-establish her authority.

"You could do that much faster with a mandoline."

"No, thanks, I prefer the knife."

Grrr! An itching in her hands made Léa realize that her patience with this girl had reached its limits.

After finishing her omelet, she went up to her apartment to take care of some paperwork. This rennet thing took her back to her first few years of vegetarianism, when she'd had to say good-bye to a whole list of products containing gelatin, a revolting substance obtained by boiling animal skins and connective tissues. But those were mainly mass-produced candies and desserts—in other words, foods she could easily do without. Not delicious, delectable cheese! She usually bought a certain brand of Emmental made with plant-based rennet—it was either fig juice or alfalfa, she wasn't sure—but the store had been out of that cheese, and she hadn't thought to check the label of this new brand. It was so easy to consume rennet without realizing it.

Were cheese and eggs even that essential? Maybe not as much as she used to think. In her search for interesting new dishes for her menu, she had recently been coming across more and more totally vegan recipes that proved delicious although they contained not the slightest bit of egg or dairy. That tiramisu made with coconut cream and cashew mascarpone, for example. She promised herself she'd do more research on the matter and give it more thought, though she didn't feel quite ready to give up certain favorite foods. And it had to be said that lacto-ovo vegetarianism was a relatively easy middle ground that held benefits for people of all ages, especially those who were only beginning to cut meat out of their diet. Anybody could become vegetarian. Just look at Mathieu.

Since their conversation at Le Chat Qui Fume after the demonstration, she hadn't been able to stop thinking about him. She picked up a sheet of paper on which she'd scribbled the characteristics of her ideal mate and reread it dubiously. How could a man be a good listener but also a good conversationalist, imbued with strong values but tolerant, protective but not macho, a bit jealous but not possessive, pragmatic but intuitive, mature but spontaneous, charismatic but unassuming, hard-working but not career-driven, friendly but not overly extroverted, and virile but in touch with his feminine side?

She threw the list of contradictions into the wastepaper basket and admitted that Mathieu did appeal to her in a certain way. Could she be developing a crush? If so, she didn't put much stock in it. Léa had grown skeptical of molecular love—just like molecular cuisine, it excited the taste buds without satisfying you and sometimes left you feeling emptier than before. She was wasting away from loneliness in this sinister hole, sure, but she wasn't about to fall into the arms of the first man who came along. And anyway, Mathieu's story about giving up meat after seeing a lion devour a gazelle in Africa was a little suspicious.

Fifteen

The last thing Mathieu had expected when he returned to La Dame Verte for lunch was a police interrogation. It was as if Léa had demanded an X-ray of his stomach so she could examine its contents! Knowing that women like repentance, he embarked upon a bloody confession, describing a past in which he had devoured not only cows, calves, sheep, chickens, and rabbits but also wild game and exotic animals such as ostriches, zebras, and llamas. To make his conversion to the green attitude more credible, he even upped the ante, posing as a former insect-eater and professing an erstwhile passion for grasshopper and cricket shish kebabs with hot sauce. Would that be enough for her? Despite being experienced at lying, he was decidedly ill at ease, and the square of vegan tiramisu sitting in front of him wasn't making him feel any better. To be polite, he would have to eat at least some of it, but he wasn't looking forward to the task.

"And now?" Léa, who had joined him at his table as he finished his meal, stopped scanning the largely empty dining room and looked back at him attentively.

He tried to act natural. "Oh, just a sardine once in a while. My doctor says you shouldn't change your diet too abruptly."

"Sure, but we can't consider fish to be an acceptable alternative to meat. If we did, we would soon empty all the oceans on the planet!"

"Uh … " These vegetarians! So stubborn, so closed-minded. Mathieu, for example, was willing to put a few lettuce leaves or a half-tomato on his plate next to his steak, but would any of them tolerate even the smallest sliver of tuna in their salad? It was clear. Getting rid of La Dame Verte was a beneficial act in the interest of public health—but that meant getting the information he had come for. He would therefore have to reassure this hysterical woman of the purity of his diet. So her compassion extended to creatures with scales and fins? Okay, whatever.

"Yes, I know," he replied. "In fact, I've been gradually replacing the fish with ground flaxseed. Did you know there's more omega-3 in a half-teaspoon of ground flaxseed than in a whole can of tuna, but without the arsenic, mercury, and lead?"

"No, I didn't." She smiled. "Where did you read that?"

"Oh, I'm interested in nutrition." This time, he knew he had her. Flipping through the women's magazines in Astrid's office wasn't always a waste of time after all.

Suddenly the little waitress, the redhead who spoke Sanskrit, approached the table. She slammed something down in front of Léa, then stormed back toward the kitchen. Baffled, Mathieu stared at the offending object—a small earthenware container of foie gras—which Léa quickly snatched up and hid under her apron.

"I … I'm sorry," she stammered. "I think there's been a misunderstanding." As all the diners looked on in astonishment, she ran after the waitress.

Misunderstanding? Yeah, right. He'd seen that the plastic wrap sealing the container had been opened, which

84

left little doubt as to the origin of the conflict: The chef of La Dame Verte—yes, this professor of food ethics—stuffed herself with foie gras in secret! As for the supposedly tranquil nature of vegetarians, the yelling coming from the kitchen spoke volumes.

Mathieu brought a spoonful of tiramisu to his mouth and forgot about his spying mission entirely. Extraordinary! He had never before experienced this—a sort of mouth orgasm, as if his salivary glands had transformed into the Trocadéro fountain.

The shouting in the kitchen stopped, and a door somewhere slammed.

Mathieu scraped the last bits of the dessert from his plate and was overcome by a sweet torpor. What if Léa were not living under a dietary dictatorship? What if she'd never had the bad idea of opening her restaurant on this site? What if she were not, in other words, the enemy to be vanquished? It had not escaped his notice that she had delicate hands, graceful wrists, and brilliantly white teeth.

He suddenly realized he was falling victim to his endorphins and got hold of himself. What if she were frigid? Hadn't he read somewhere that certain puritan vegetarian pioneers in the United States had advocated sexual abstinence, and that the most extreme among them had compared an erection to a ship's mast towering over a grave? In any case, with the iron deficiency she surely had, it wouldn't be long before her teeth fell out, her hair turned white, and her skin became soft and flabby. These vegetarians didn't realize they needed to be protected from themselves for the sake of their own health.

A few minutes later, Léa stepped back into the dining room and made an announcement to all the diners. "I would like to apologize. We had a little problem in the kitchen, but it's been resolved." She managed a strained smile. "We will be serving complimentary coffee."

As Léa came back toward his table, Mathieu noticed that she was quite pale.

"What happened?"

"Don't tell anyone," she murmured, "but Pervenche just went out the back door."

"Huh?"

"We had a few words." She bit her thumb. "It seems I've fired her."

Vegetarian but not vegetative! He'd better watch out …

"She found my foie gras. I tried to explain that it was essential for the recipe I'm working on, but she wouldn't listen. So stubborn!"

"Recipe?"

"Didn't I tell you about my vegetarian foie gras project?" Léa went to the cash register to take a customer's payment.

Vegetarian foie gras—yuck! It was true that she'd said something about it the first time they'd met, but he hadn't taken her seriously. After a moment, he approached the counter wearing a suitable expression.

"I'm sorry about your assistant."

"Thanks." She bit her thumb again. "I don't know what I'm going to do."

This was the moment he'd been waiting for! "Any news about your loan?"

She furrowed her brow. "My loan?"

"The one you were telling me about the other day."

"No, not yet."

"I know quite a few bank directors because of my work. If I can be of any help … "

"Thank you, but my application is quite solid."

"I'm sure it is," he said. Who did she think she was? Bill Gates's niece, perhaps? "How much do I owe you?"

"Fifteen euros." She took the bill he held out and rummaged through the drawer for the change. "But I really appreciate your offer."

As Mathieu drove back to the offices of Nedelec Pork, he wondered what to do. The poor girl was in dire straits, and he didn't want to be the one to hammer the first nail in her coffin. It could upset his digestion. And then, after all, that blockhead Jean-Sylvain was right—all they had to do was find another location for their museum. To be honest, the best thing would be to forget about the project altogether. Sure, it was his baby, but he was feeling less and less enthusiastic, and …

Screeech! At the last moment, he noticed the red light and braked. Holy Moses! What was happening to him? Was it possible that this vegetarian food was having an effect on his brain? Was it interfering with his aggressiveness and ability to produce adrenaline, both of which were essential for survival in the business world? What about his career? And his promotion to general manager? He wasn't Bambi's little brother, damn it all!

By the time he turned off his engine in the Nedelec Pork parking lot, he had overcome his moment of weakness. He went straight to Auguste's HQ. The big boss listened attentively as Mathieu reported on his mission.

"A vegetarian foie gras! These four-stomached ruminants are even more unhinged than I thought! So you couldn't get the information?"

"She must have sensed I was an infiltrating carnivore."

Auguste didn't bat an eye. "In that case … " He grabbed his telephone and dialed a number. "Jean-Sylvain? Could you come to my office? Yes, right now." He put the receiver down with a crafty grin. "Given what we're going to be spending on our museum, I don't know of a banker in the whole city of Rennes who would refuse to do us a little favor. This doesn't shock you, I hope?"

"Are you kidding?" Léa would have to close up shop, but Mathieu had nothing to feel bad about—the idea to put pressure on the banks had come from Auguste.

The CEO moved on to another topic. "You've probably noticed that Astrid is a little low these days. She's still thinking about her breakup with her ex—that nincompoop!—even though I think it was the smartest decision she's made in her whole life." He looked meaningfully at Mathieu. "She feels real friendship for you. I know that you're very busy with your work, but … "

"Yes?"

"Maybe you could take her out once in a while. Get her mind off things."

"Uh … sure."

His boss smiled at him gratefully. "She's a very reserved girl, but she's worth knowing. You'll see." And he winked. "Take her to a nice restaurant. It's on me."

Sixteen

Dressed in a sober business jacket and a pencil skirt that fell just above her knees, Léa entered the bank and asked to see the representative who was handling her file. The businesswoman look wasn't really her style, but she'd made a special effort for this appointment since the future of La Dame Verte was at stake. After waiting fifteen minutes, Léa was on tenterhooks when the banker finally appeared, shook her hand, and asked her to follow him.

"Your application is very well put together. I must congratulate you on that."

She hated the lecherous look he gave her as he pointed to the chair on the other side of the table. "I put a lot of work into it."

"And it shows." He opened a folder, glanced in it, and then closed it with a solemn expression. "Ms. Rystel, I'm going to be frank with you. Despite the thoroughness of your application, we are not one hundred percent convinced by your project."

"What!" She grabbed the arm of her chair. "Because it's a vegetarian restaurant?"

"The clientele you reach is marginal."

"Marginal?"

"Let's not get excited. I meant limited."

"But more and more people have been coming in!" She took the folder and pulled out a chart—though the figures were a bit doctored, it was true. "See, right here!"

The man shrugged his shoulders. "If your restaurant were in the downtown area, I wouldn't say no. You know better than me that when it comes to the restaurant business, it's location, location, location."

"But I can't afford the rents downtown!"

"We've examined your application thoroughly, believe me."

Yet her application was bulletproof. "All right, but what if I asked for less? Let's say ten thousand euros instead of fifteen. With ten thousand, I could cover my next few payments and replenish my cash flow. I promise you won't regret it."

"Sorry."

"Five thousand?"

"Ms. Rystel, my supervisors and I wish you all the best in your future endeavors," he said, pushing the folder over to her.

Léa felt a hot anger bubbling up inside her. "Where are your supervisors? I demand to speak to the bank manager!"

"Calm down, Ms. Rystel, there's no need to light your Molotov cocktails."

He seemed to be enjoying the situation. She wanted to punch him. "What are you implying?"

"You heard what I said. As a ringleader of the vegetarian movement, you won't have an easy time finding a bank willing to lend you this sum. At least not here in Rennes."

She stood up. "Ringleader? You … you … " She raised her hand.

Panicking, the man pressed a button to call for a security guard, forcing Léa to flee for the door, past a group of astonished bank customers.

Raindrops crashed against her face. The gray sky, the fronts of buildings, the expressionless eyes of people on the street—everything struck her as hostile. Ringleader! She began to wonder whether she wasn't the victim of a conspiracy. She should have set up her restaurant in Ghent, Belgium, where 15 percent of the restaurants were vegetarian. But no, with her naive desire to help spread awareness, she had chosen Rennes—Rennes, the capital of pork products ever since Parisian technocrats had decided in the 1960s to make the region into a meat factory. Pig farms had sprung up like mushrooms all over Brittany … a piggening that could apparently be stopped by nothing, least of all by the dishes at La Dame Verte.

She made her way up the street. Was it a crime to stray from the beaten path? Her ability to withstand failure— which had always been good, this ability that was even more important than talent for anyone who strived to achieve a truly meaningful goal—was reaching its limits. Nothing but problems, obstacles, humiliations! Had she been wrong? Should she have finished her degree and become an art teacher, as her family had urged her to? She could have, but where was the passion in that? Even if it meant being alone and borrowing money, she'd felt the need to follow a dream, to pursue an ideal. Like any other person, she had her own strengths, a potential that she alone could tap into, the ability to create something unique, even if on a modest scale, and nobody on earth would detract her from this goal. Her mother had made that mistake, renouncing a promising career as a painter to become an actuary in an insurance company, and Léa would not make the same error.

Arming herself with renewed courage, she went to prepare for the lunch service but became more depressed than ever upon entering the kitchen of La Dame Verte. Without the *thwack, thwack, thwack* of Pervenche's knife, the room was as silent as a tomb. Next to the sink, two crates of vegetables sadly awaited their final hour. Even the cooking utensils, organized a bit too carefully, had a lifeless and resigned air about them. As if the place had lost part of its charm, its soul.

~

Lunch was drawing to a close when a middle-aged customer with a gray bouffant approached the cash register.

"If you don't mind, could I ask what you used to replace the snails in that dish?"

Her round, friendly face was familiar to Léa. She'd already seen her in the restaurant two or three times. Léa forced herself to smile. "Oyster mushrooms sautéed in a garlic butter sauce. They have the same texture."

The woman's look of amazement cheered her up somewhat.

"Then just replace the shells with mini puff pastries, and you're good to go."

Léa took the woman's company meal vouchers and opened the cash register drawer. The sight of the empty compartments brought her mood back down. To think that she'd imagined her veggie escargots could amuse the inhabitants of Rennes in this rainy weather!

"What happened to your friend who usually waits tables?" asked the woman.

Léa realized that she really did miss Pervenche and became sadder still. "She's … um … on vacation." Her face fell, and she struggled to hold back her tears.

"What's the matter?" asked the customer.

"Nothing. I'm just very tired."

"Are you sure?"

"Yes."

"Well, I'm glad to hear that. I truly admire what you do. And I'm not even a vegetarian."

"Ah, really?" Léa got herself under control. "Don't worry, there's nothing wrong with that. In fact, I think it's great that non-vegetarians are taking an interest in plant-based cuisine, even if it's just once a week, or once a month."

The customer patted her gray hair, then looked at Léa intently. "Can I make a confession? The first time I came here, I was kind of scared."

"Why?"

"Well, so many people had warned me about vegetarians. And so I imagined you people as harsh and intolerant."

"And we are!" Léa joked. Like any self-respecting vegetarian, she had a rejoinder at the ready for this type of situation. "At least we were in the seventies, when we lived in a symbiotic relationship with the goats on our communes in the wilderness. But times have changed. Vegetarianism is no longer just for animal-rights supporters or followers of Eastern philosophy. More and more people are choosing it for health reasons or because of the greenhouse effect."

Seeing the woman's surprise, Léa felt impelled to elaborate on her last point. "Eighteen percent of greenhouse gas emissions come from livestock farming. That's more than transportation. It may sound strange, but a vegetarian who drives a four-by-four pollutes less than a carnivore who rides a bicycle. I know people who have gone vegetarian for that reason alone."

Léa didn't know whether it was due to the pressure of the previous few days, but she couldn't summon the restraint she usually practiced when talking about the meat industry. "Furthermore, if people knew about the barbarian methods used by meat producers, three-fourths of them would become vegetarian!"

"Uh … yes, I'm sure you're right." The customer glanced

at her watch uneasily and began to move toward the door. "Look at the time! I've got to run."

"Wouldn't you like some coffee?"

"No, thank you. I'm going to be late. Bye!"

Léa cursed herself. A lost sheep had been looking for the right path, and she had to go and ruin everything with a stupid anti-meat comment! Had she forgotten that the region of Brittany produced fourteen million pigs per year for a human population of only around three million—in other words, more than four pigs per inhabitant? The chances were high that someone in this woman's family worked at a slaughterhouse or for a manufacturer in the pork sector.

In any case, the situation had required more tact. Léa thought of her own journey to vegetarianism. As a child, she had often wondered what happened between the time a cow entered a slaughterhouse and the moment it exited the factory in a can of corned beef, like in *Tintin in America*. But it was only at the age of twenty-five that she'd had the courage to dig deeper. She watched *Earthlings* on the Internet. This documentary, narrated by Joaquin Phoenix, convinced her to stop eating meat, but it was not necessarily for everyone since the images were very disturbing. This was why a subtler, more epicurean approach was also needed. By including vegetarian fare on their menus, certain chefs did more to promote this way of eating than Veggie Pride; she was sure of it. This was what she had wanted to pursue, but La Dame Verte was at the end of its rope. A few more days like this, and …

The door opened again and the same customer reappeared. She seemed distressed. She approached the counter hesitantly. "I wanted to tell you—I work at Nedelec Pork. And there's something you should know about this site."

Seventeen

Although he was in his prime, and he'd never had complaints about his performance, Mathieu decided he would need to start taking ginseng. Astrid had just curled up against him for the umpteenth time that night and stuck her tongue in his ear with no effort to hide her intentions. What energy! That said, it was welcome news, for nothing scared him more than sentimental blah blah: long kisses, deep looks into each other's eyes. Astrid's tongue left his ear, and her hand brushed against his navel as she propped herself up on one elbow.

"Mathieu?"

He prepared himself for another indecent proposal. "Yes?"

"Do you love me?"

Did she smoke joints made from Harlequin novels or something? A few hours earlier, in the ultra-chic restaurant they'd dined at, he had indeed felt something. But was it love? Wasn't it more likely the excitement caused by Astrid's foot rubbing against his own under the table? Or the fit of tenderness that had come over him when he'd imagined having the statistical two and a half children with her?

Anyway, what did it mean to love? Wasn't love something like the Loch Ness monster, which everyone talked about but nobody had seen? No, it must exist. Otherwise, why had it been the topic of so many conversations and so much art for centuries? Why had all his friends, since high school, annoyed him with talk about their love lives? He had to admit that he was unfortunately suffering from a serious case of romantic impotence that couldn't be cured by any little blue pills. He would never experience the excitement or true ecstasy of love, for his genitalia were his only love organs. Yet these organs were able to boost his career up toward previously unhoped-for summits. Trying to block the horrible candy-box decor of Astrid's bedroom from his field of vision, he adopted an appropriate expression.

"Yes, I love you."

She batted her eyelashes. "I'm so happy! Do you know what I want to do?"

"We'll do anything you like, as long as you promise to let me sleep at least two hours before going to work."

"Ingrate!" She tousled his hair. "No, I'd like to have dinner at your place sometime soon. I'm free on Wednesday."

Dinner at his place? On Wednesday? What an idea! It was early Tuesday morning, which meant he had only one evening to prepare for the big event. His apartment smelled like a hamster cage, the floor was strewn with dirty laundry, and the chemical formula that could dissolve the buildup in his bathtub remained to be discovered. Some of his moving boxes hadn't even been opened yet. Basically, it was the last place on earth he would want to set foot if he were a woman.

But disappointing Astrid didn't fit into his career plan. He would have to go to the supermarket on his lunch break to buy cleaning products and ingredients for a dinner of some kind so his place would be ready for another "romantic" night.

∽

As he entered the parking lot of the local mega-market, he was surprised to see Norbert and a few of his minions handing out free veggie burgers across from a fast-food restaurant. Having taken the precaution of lowering his visor, he drove past them slowly. All around a vehicle that looked like a food truck, the plant-eaters had set up signs covered with their idiotic slogans. No sign of Léa.

Rubbing a sore muscle, Mathieu thought back to his night with Astrid. She would never get him a top score on the True Love Test, but at least she wouldn't endanger his mental health. Léa, on the other hand, was the type of chick who would send you to the shrink. It had already happened to him with a couple of intellectual omnivore girlfriends, and he wasn't about to repeat the experience with a vegetarian one.

He parked and got himself a shopping cart. Supermarkets fascinated him. As a marketing director, he could glean precious information by wandering through the aisles, examining the shelves, and observing consumers interacting with the products. But he would have to save that for another time because he now had only twenty minutes to do his shopping.

Skirting around the line of cash registers, he ran over the ingredients for roast pork ratatouille in his mind. It was a recipe that he could usually make a success of using his trusty old pressure-cooker, the one his mother had given him when he left home to study at that second-rate business school.

Eighteen

After an hour of handing out burgers in the parking lot with Norbert, Max, Lorelei, and other members of the Rennes Vegetarian Society, Léa stole away and headed into the shopping center. She sat down at the bar of a café adjacent to the supermarket, ordered a coffee, and, in a very dejected mood, watched the ballet of shopping carts maneuvering in front of the supermarket's cash registers. There had been a time, before she had tired of the two brands of soy steaks that fought an endless duel at the back of the organic section, that she, too, had frequented these food factories. Scrutinizing the labels to check for gelatin or other animal-based additives (the manufacturers had a talent for slipping them into the most unlikely products) had been her favorite hobby back then, but she had grown weary of it over time and switched to other, less depressing reading material and different distribution channels.

Suddenly, her heart jumped in her chest. Wasn't that Mathieu she'd just seen go by, in a business suit? She realized that he definitely had an effect on her. But what was his story? Was he really a vegetarian? Or was he a UFO, one of those "unidentified flexitarian objects" who had been sighted more and more often lately: people who called themselves vegetarians but who, making "exceptions" for holidays, gorged themselves on turkey at Christmas? After a brief hesitation, her curiosity got the better of her.

She didn't have to follow him for long. Like a shark attracted by the scent of blood, Mathieu went straight to the meat section and set his sights on a monstrously large pork roast.

Should she show herself? She was having an off day, and she felt about as attractive as a tree stump, but what did that matter now, after this horrendous discovery? She emerged from her hiding spot behind a promotional shelf stocked with andouille sausages.

"Hey, there!"

Mathieu jumped. "Léa!"

"I noticed you from a distance." She stared at the pork roast he still held in his hand. "Oh! Perhaps I'm interrupting you … "

"Not at all."

"Don't be afraid. I'm not going to faint."

He put the evidence in his cart. "Uh … I'm having carnivore friends over for dinner."

She would respond as an activist, she decided, so he wouldn't see that he'd disappointed her on a personal level. "You don't have to explain. It's just that since you talked about eating sardines once in a while, I thought you were a pesco-vegetarian."

He shifted his weight nervously from one foot to the other. "Okay, okay. I'm more like a neo-vegetarian. An omnivore interested in a more plant-based diet, you could say."

"So, unlike what you told me, you still eat meat?"

"Less and less." He showed her the eggplant, zucchini,

and bell peppers in his cart. "See? The ingredients for my ratatouille."

She gave him a bitter smile. "It's funny—whenever I meet carnivores, they tell me they're eating less meat. And yet meat consumption is still on the rise. Doesn't quite add up, does it?"

Mathieu was clearly very uncomfortable. He lowered his head. "It was stupid of me, but I was afraid you would think I was a monster if you knew that I sometimes still eat meat."

If he was trying to pull her into an overly personal territory, he was going to be disappointed. "Pfft! You think all vegetarians are stubborn ideologists who are unable to have normal friendships with non-vegetarians, is that it?"

"No, I didn't say that."

"But you just said you were afraid I would see you as a monster! For your information, we respect individual freedoms. Including the freedom to eat meat." She raised her voice. "You don't have to pretend to be something you're not!"

Heads began turning in their direction. From Mathieu's expression, she could see that he was terrified of a scandal. A pseudo-vegetarian and a coward, too! She hoped his roast had been repackaged. It was a common enough practice, even in large stores such as this one, to rewrap expired meat with a new sell-by date, sometimes with serious consequences for the customer's digestive system.

Suddenly Léa saw Lorelei, the former model, coming toward her with a swinging stride, her beautiful mass of auburn hair waving behind her. Despite his distress, Mathieu's eyes grew as big as saucers as she approached.

"You okay, Léa?" Lorelei asked in her breathy voice. "We've been looking for you everywhere."

A dedicated vegan, Lorelei rejected all forms of animal exploitation. She categorically refused to let leather, wool, or silk come into contact with her precious epidermis. Was it this purity that made Léa feel so envious, or was it because, despite having reached the advanced age of forty, Lorelei still had a killer body? She wasn't sure, but as she made the introductions, she realized this was a good opportunity to stick it to Mathieu even further.

"Lorelei, Mathieu." Léa looked at Lorelei. "I don't know if you saw each other, but Mathieu was at Veggie Pride. He was just telling me that he's not vegetarian anymore. He's flexitarian."

"Flexitarian?"

"As in flexible. He still eats meat, but very little. Just a gigantic pork roast from time to time, to go with his ratatouille."

Lorelei seemed ill at ease. "Léa, we have a rush going on at the stand. We really need you back there." She looked at Mathieu, or rather what remained of him. "If you want to try a veggie burger, we're in the parking lot."

"Yeah, and you can get burgers made of pure beef just across the way," Léa added with a look of total innocence.

Nineteen

Back in the lobby of the Nedelec Pork offices, Mathieu pounded furiously on the elevator call button. That damned vegetarian had made him grovel in public like a potato bug, crawl into the ground like a common root vegetable! If she hadn't caught him red-handed in a supermarket belonging to a customer of his company, he would have responded to her vile attack by telling her where he worked, just to see her face.

The doors of the elevator opened to reveal Auguste. With no warning, Auguste wrapped his arms around Mathieu with the strength of a boa constrictor, to the point that his employee gasped for breath. When the embrace relaxed, Mathieu beheld the extraordinary sight of the CEO's face inches away from his own, tears welling up in his eyes. So, Astrid kept absolutely no secrets from her parents? Or did Auguste have spies in his employ? And how would Jean-Sylvain react to the news of Mathieu getting it on with his cousin? For a moment he thought Daddy-in-Law was about to advise him on the color of their baby's layette, but no, he exited the elevator in silence after clapping him on the shoulder. Mathieu stood there in confusion, taking stock of all the expectations weighing upon him.

An hour later, he was looking at a market study when his cell phone vibrated in his pocket: a text message from Léa, inviting him to taste her foie gras the next evening. So! She really had it out for him.

Too annoyed to go back to his work, Mathieu looked over at Arlette, who was coming and going behind the glass window that separated their offices. What was up with his secretary? He was still disturbed by their last conversation. Arlette had questioned the ethics of their work and spoken of the cruelty of slaughterhouses. Cruelty was a part of nature, he'd replied. It wasn't the fault of the meat industry. For proof, she need only remember that animals have been devouring each other since the dawn of time. Moreover, you couldn't compare the fate of an animal raised to be eaten with that of a wild animal. A cow cannot miss a meadow if she has never been to one, for example.

But Arlette had dismantled all his arguments. According to her, nature had nothing to do with it since these animals were produced artificially and in absurd numbers. For example, there were now two billion cattle on earth.

Mathieu had ended the debate by telling Arlette it wasn't their fault if the French were the descendants of Obelix and had a passion for meat in their genes. But Arlette worried him. It was possible that she continued to frequent La Dame Verte, or even that she'd been brainwashed by the vegetarians. And speaking of animal suffering was one thing—but what about human suffering? She should think of herself first and foremost, since this kind of talk could lead to unemployment.

His telephone rang. Auguste wanted to see him immediately. Wondering about a possible connection to his appointment as general manager, Mathieu scaled the stairs two by two. But his mood was soon dampened.

The tension could have been cut with a knife. The head honcho was seated at his desk, flanked by Jean-Sylvain and an Astrid who was clearly light years away from their romp of the night before.

"I've had a phone call from the president of that organization. A man named Norbert," said Auguste.

"The vegetarians, you mean?"

"Yes. They're threatening to hold a demonstration in protest of our pork museum project."

"What's wrong with that? Let them do it—it'll be free publicity for us."

"I don't think so," objected Astrid. "The guy told Daddy that we'd better stop harassing Léa Rystel and look for another site."

"Yes, he even said something about suing me!" said Auguste indignantly, pounding his fist down on the desk hard enough to make his porcelain piggy bank jump.

"Daddy, calm down."

"Calm down? This project is a strategic one for Nedelec Pork and the entire sector! I will not let a band of two-legged ruminants stand in its way!"

He clutched his chest, seized by a coughing fit. Astrid hurried to get him an effervescent tablet in a glass of water. Clearly, his heart was giving him more and more trouble these days, but Auguste couldn't bring himself to step down just yet. He insisted on continuing the meeting.

Jean-Sylvain, whose cologne could have downed an insect in mid-flight, added his two cents. "What I'd like to know is how they found out about it. Someone from our side must have squealed. There's no other way." He cast a sidelong glance at Mathieu. "You know these people well, Mathieu. Perhaps you have an idea?"

The jackass was accusing him? While *he* was the one doing all the hard work? Ignoring him, Mathieu turned to Auguste.

"Saying that I know them well is going pretty far. I ate at the restaurant twice. At my own risk and peril, I might add. You know as well as I do that these people are cannibals."

"Cannibals?"

"Yes. Since they don't ingest any animal protein, they consume the protein of their own muscles. It's self-cannibalism. I noticed a loss of muscle mass myself after those two meals." It wasn't true, but a famous anti-vegetarian nutritionist, who thought of himself as the alpha and omega-3 of a healthy diet, had recently been shouting this on all the airwaves.

Auguste looked perturbed. "That's right—you have shown great courage. Myself, I would be unable to eat the slop they serve there. Not even if you deep-fried it."

Mathieu shot a self-satisfied look at Jean-Sylvain. The rookie could put that in his pipe and smoke it.

But then Astrid ruined everything. "I wonder if it wasn't Arlette who informed them. I know she's had lunch there several times."

Well! He knew Astrid couldn't stand his secretary, but he hadn't anticipated such a frontal attack. That foolish Arlette! He'd told her to be discreet.

"Jean-Sylvain." Auguste looked at his nephew. "I want you to begin negotiations with Léa Rystel, on the double! Take out your checkbook if you have to. As for Arlette … " His hand slammed down on the table like a guillotine, chilling Mathieu's blood. Given the strange attitude of his right-hand woman lately, her responsibility for this information leak was clear. But with the general manager position and Astrid's favors at stake, saving Private Arlette could ruin his career.

"Just a moment," he said.

"Yes?" replied Auguste impatiently.

"Well … if Arlette has made a mistake, it's my responsibility to bear." He couldn't believe his ears. Whoever was talking in his place must be a real loser. "Léa Rystel is holding a foie gras tasting event tomorrow evening … ”

“Foie gras!” exclaimed Astrid and Jean-Sylvain at the same time.

“Yes, a vegetarian version. These people are maniacs, believe me, but I could attempt a last-ditch negotiation with her.” He looked at Astrid and saw from her expression that she wasn't opposed to postponing their dinner if it was for a good cause.

～

Why, after sending the text message, had Léa called Mathieu to make sure he would come to her tasting event? Was the poor thing so deficient in iron that she was after his blood? Or was it a strategy to vegetarianize him and pull him over to the green side of the Force? In either case, she was going to fall flat on her face. He had received full permission from Auguste to settle the question of La Dame Verte. If the nut demanded money in exchange for closing down her salad bar, the old man was willing to go along with it. The important thing was for her to get out, and quick.

He parked and looked warily at the brightly lit windows of La Dame Verte. Soon after, another car parked across from his own, and a beautiful woman emerged—it was that Lorelei he'd met earlier at the supermarket. The man at the wheel was none other than that blithering old nuisance of a Norbert. More people—undoubtedly all ringleaders in the movement—arrived in the next few minutes, which only increased Mathieu's agitation. But he couldn't turn back now.

He stepped into the restaurant and saw that Léa had gone all out: white tablecloths, bouquets of flowers on the counter, jazz drifting from speakers. It would have been an enchanting ambiance, if only there weren't so many vegetarians. It was amazing what bad vibrations these aficionados of Kamut wheat and beefsteak tomatoes could give off.

Suddenly, Léa appeared before him. Her blonde hair shone, and she wore a black-and-white checkered dress that left none of her shoulders' anemic whiteness to the imagination. Rather than look daggers at him, she smiled benevolently above the tray of full champagne flutes she held in her hands.

"I'm glad you were able to come."

Skinny but ravishing, he had to admit.

"Uh … to be honest, I was a bit surprised to get your invitation." He didn't try to hide his discomfort. "Especially after the pork roast yesterday … "

"Water under the bridge. Let's look ahead to the future."

"A vegetarian future, right?"

"A girl can dream. Champagne? I'm liquidating the wine cellar." She tried to smile, but the corners of her mouth wouldn't quite rise. "I'm liquidating everything, in fact."

Was she going to close the restaurant? Wonderful, providential! He managed a look of sympathy. "More problems?"

She shrugged, and Mathieu was pleasantly surprised to see that her shoulders actually had a nice roundness to them. She wasn't so skinny after all, just slender.

"Yeah. It looks like I'll have to close by the end of the month, if things keep going the way they are now. And I've also learned that certain people want me out of here."

"Oh?" Mathieu's stomach did a somersault.

"But let's not dwell on depressing topics."

He relaxed a bit—she didn't seem to suspect him. "I have to admit, this restaurant was an ambitious idea from the beginning," she said. "It turns out Homer was right. You don't win friends with salad."

"Come again?"

"Homer Simpson. You know, when his daughter Lisa goes vegetarian … "

Lisa was the smartest of the Simpsons, but she was snotty. Mathieu had always preferred Bart—a real carnivore, that one. "I used to watch the show, but I must have missed that episode. Say … " He was going to ask her the exact date of La Dame Verte's closure when a voice interrupted him.

"Mathieu! You, here?"

His blood froze. But to his relief, it was only Norbert.

Léa seemed to jump on the opportunity to excuse herself. "I have some things to take care of in the kitchen. Norbert, can you keep an eye on him for me?"

"Keep an eye on me?"

"Don't worry, we're not going to eat you." Léa smiled as she turned to go.

What did she mean by that? Mathieu would have loved to sneak out, but the president of the Rennes Vegetarian Society began introducing him to other guests as a new recruit. To his surprise, he noticed the lovely Lorelei gazing at him rather intently. What did she want with him? There was no chance to find out because a group had formed around him and Norbert, and a discussion on anti-vegetarian prejudices was starting up.

"I don't know why, just because I'm vegetarian, I'm supposed to stop killing mosquitos," said a girl wearing a heavy-metal T-shirt and big black boots.

"I know, it's unfair," complained another guest. "And if an omnivore doesn't smoke or drink, people compliment them on their self-discipline, but if it's a vegetarian, they're accused of being obsessed with their health or not knowing how to have fun."

Mathieu finished his glass and chuckled to himself. These poor creatures never stopped whimpering and setting themselves up as martyrs to the vegetable cause.

"Oh, boo hoo!" broke in a guy called Max. He added vehemently, "When will you see that we need to take action to get rid of the meat industry?"

"I think we've already had this conversation," interrupted Norbert. "You know that a violent attitude will get us nowhere." He looked around at the group and smiled. "Let me tell you instead about the peaceful panda. The journal *Nature* has just published an article about how this amiable creature used to be a carnivore."

"But I thought they ate nothing but bamboo!" exclaimed Lorelei.

"Yes, twenty pounds a day. However, although their genome contains only the enzymes of their flesh-eating ancestors, they learned to subcontract the digestion of cellulose to their gut bacteria."

Mathieu couldn't resist the temptation to antagonize him. "Okay, but then how do you explain the existence of carnivorous plants? If even plants eat meat, how can we justify our position?"

"That has nothing to do with it. And anyway, carnivorous plants are a kind of evolutionary mistake."

You're the evolutionary mistake! Mathieu thought.

Just then, the clinking of a fork against a crystal wine glass signaled the beginning of the tasting. The group crowded around a large table laid with baskets of bread, several bottles of Sauternes and Armagnac, and an antique silver platter with a dome cover.

Léa switched off the music and cleared her throat. "If you allow, I will begin with a statement made recently by a columnist in *La Gazette Parisienne*. And I quote: 'Who wrote *The Red and the Black*, an animal or a man? Since no duck has ever written a literary masterpiece, I say we can eat them.' End quote."

Léa paused as a few indignant reactions rose up from the group. "Personally, I prefer living ducks and would not venture to establish a hierarchy among the species. But tonight I have good news for the ducks and also for people who love the taste of foie gras but don't have a superiority complex toward other beings."

She lifted the cover off the platter with a flourish, and the group began clapping. Léa had even gone so far as to reproduce the yellowish hue of a real block of foie gras.

"You can already find a vegetarian foie gras at the organic shops," she said, "but what you see here is nothing like that pale imitation. The taste and texture, as you will soon see, are very close to the real thing. To prove it, I have devised a little test. Mathieu?"

Damn! What the hell was she—

"Mathieu, please?"

Several heads turned in his direction, filling him with terror.

"Mathieu is a neo-vegetarian," continued Léa, "which means that he's transitioning and sometimes still eats meat. Right, Mathieu?"

"Uh ... yes, that's right." It wasn't against the law, after all.

"And that's perfectly normal. Most of us here went through that same process ourselves. Mathieu, could I ask you whether you sometimes also still eat foie gras?"

"Well ... only at Christmastime. You know, pressure from the family ... "

"No need to explain—this is a free country, after all. Could you come up to the table, please?"

He saw he had no choice. A few moments later, two plates were placed in front of him. Each contained a round, beige-ivory slice with a smooth-looking texture.

"One of these is traditional foie gras from a duck, while the other is my vegetarian version. Can you identify the real one?"

He shot Léa a spiteful look. Blast and damnation! Now he knew why she had insisted on his being here.

With dozens of eyes trained on him, he set himself to the task. He could not conceal his surprise: Both samples were rich and flavorful, with a slightly grainy texture at the end. He cleansed his palate with a bit of Sauternes and tasted them again. This time he noticed that one of the samples had a somewhat longer finish. He pointed at it with his fork.

"This one."

Léa beamed like an eight-year-old on a sugar high. "I have a confession to make—this was a trap. Both of them are vegetarian! You couldn't tell?"

"Uh … no."

Thunderous applause erupted among the guests, and Mathieu hid his fury behind a smile. Abusing his disadvantaged position to fool him about the quality of the merchandise! What a revolting thing to do.

But he had to admit he was amazed. If these counterfeiters managed to imitate meat products to such perfection, foie gras and pork producers would have to begin putting serial numbers on their output. Perhaps meat substitutes were the future of the agrifoods industry after all.

A little later, as the guests were sampling the foie gras, mingling and chatting, Mathieu looked around for Léa. Although she'd used him as a guinea pig in that scandalous way, he found he couldn't stay angry with her. How strange! Was he suffering from Stockholm syndrome? Could he be falling for her?

No, it was the other way around. *She* had a thing for *him*. Otherwise, why would she have wanted revenge? He took comfort in this thought.

He mixed among the guests and finally found her deep in conversation with the gastroenterologist he had gone to, that Julien what's-his-face, who, to his great surprise, had ended up prescribing him group psychotherapy to cure his stomach pains! The doctor's expression suggested that he was confessing romantic feelings to Léa. Mathieu felt his fists clenching. Was this what those who knew the mysteries of love called jealousy? And just like in accounting, where the existence of a liability presupposed the existence of an asset, was it possible that a negative feeling—his hostility toward Julien—was proof that he felt something for Léa that he had never felt for any other woman?

Mathieu retreated to a corner of the room to think. He had come here to make sure the restaurant would close. That was as good as done, and the Nedelecs never even needed to know that he hadn't had to work for it. He could leave now, his mission accomplished and a bright career ahead of him. But ... he didn't quite want to leave.

He closed his eyes to concentrate, as he sometimes did when he was in his office and had to make a difficult decision. He knew he needed to bring his focus back to the bright future waiting for him in the meat industry. But all he could think of was Léa's beautiful hair and her soft white shoulder, a pink bra strap peeking out from inside her dress.

His eyes flew open as he realized how insane it was to daydream of her. She would never accept him once she found out that he worked with her enemies and, even worse, was the one spearheading the pork museum project. Unless he were to make a full confession now, before she found out about it from someone else. He would need a helmet and a bulletproof vest, but it seemed the only way to get out of this sticky situation.

As Mathieu turned back to the dining room, he nearly collided with Lorelei, who was coming through the kitchen door at the same moment.

"Here you are!" She smiled. "I've been looking for you everywhere."

Twenty

Léa suppressed a giggle. Julien—he was so amusing—had just confessed to another fall from the wagon. Apparently he had gone wild at a medical conference and eaten several slices of lamb. A desperate case, she thought: a visceral inaptitude for vegetarianism that afflicted a small percentage of people. The inaptitude of the rest was cultural.

Speaking of hopeless cases, where was Mathieu? Had he already left? Léa got rid of Julien and looked around. She hoped he wasn't taking her little trick too badly—her goal hadn't been to humiliate Mathieu, only to make him pay for his lies. She was undeniably growing attached, however, in spite of the red flags that kept popping up. He seemed respectable enough, at least outwardly, yet she really didn't know that much about him. For example, he'd said he worked in IT but had never mentioned which company he was with. No way to find out on the sly either, since she didn't even know his last name!

But she was even more curious about his love life. Of course, he'd seemed to accept her invitation to the tasting event without any difficulty—a good sign, since a man in a relationship might not have been free in the evening, even during the week. Yet the thing with the pork roast was strange. Her culinary sixth sense told her that his kitchen skills went no further than boiled eggs. So what was he doing with a roast? Or, more important, *who* was he planning to make it for? Anyway, could she even go out with a meat-eater, much less settle down with one? She thought for a moment. If they kept separate cookware and refrigerators, the idea didn't seem entirely implausible.

She finally spotted him drinking champagne with Lorelei near the counter. They both seemed to be enjoying themselves. And, to Léa's despair, the former model was looking more beautiful than ever. Not only was Lorelei a virtuoso of foundation and lipstick, she was also the best-dressed woman in Rennes. The scruffiest of Lorelei's clothes made Léa's nicest outfits—for example, the dress she was wearing tonight—look like rejects from the Salvation Army.

Léa scrutinized Mathieu's face worriedly, searching for clues. Were his eyes shining? Were his facial muscles relaxed? What did his body language reveal? In less than a second, the answers to these questions were processed through the filters of her personal database and compared against thousands of files. Faced with the alarming result, she hid behind a group of people to observe the pair.

Suddenly she saw Lorelei undo the top buttons of her blouse as a fascinated Mathieu leaned forward to take a look. Calm down, Léa told herself; she's just showing him her new, 100-percent ethical bra made with recycled pine fibers and vegetable dye, as she's already done with half the population of Rennes. Still, it was too much. Léa turned and made her way to the other side of the restaurant.

At the end of the evening, Norbert, Max, Lorelei, Julien, and Mathieu stayed behind to help Léa clean up. Mathieu seemed to be trying to distance himself from Lorelei and to get closer to Léa. Léa gave him the cold shoulder, but under the surface, she was more confused than ever. Had she been wrong about his intentions? Had he flirted with Lorelei only to get closer to her, in some kind of complicated multi-step seduction strategy?

As everyone was leaving, Lorelei grabbed hold of Mathieu's arm. "I'm counting on you to take me home!"

"Uh ... of course," he mumbled in reply.

Léa clenched her teeth. Spineless! Truly, she never wanted to see him again.

As she locked the front door, the silence of the large empty room came crashing down on her. She tried to fix her thoughts on her sweet Charline, sleeping upstairs, but that image brought her no comfort. At least now she knew that Mathieu lived alone. Otherwise, Lorelei could never have gotten her hooks into him so easily.

Yet this consolation was so small, and her feeling of abandonment so heavy, that Léa leaned back against the door and covered her face with her hands to escape the vision of her future, a depressing mixture of financial ruin and bankruptcy of the heart. Would she end up in the street, as certain gossips had predicted?

Just then, a few timid knocks sounded on the door behind her. She opened it and was very surprised to find none other than Mathieu himself. He had moved away from the door, back down the two front steps, and appeared to be trying to shrink down inside of himself. Although excited that he had returned, she saw no reason to make things easy for him.

"Hey, look who's here! Lorelei's chauffeur."

"I told her I'd lost my car keys." He looked up at her with apprehensive eyes. "There's something I have to tell you."

"If it's about Lorelei, you don't have to explain. It's none of my business what you do in your private life."

"No, no, it has nothing to do with her. I … " He bit his lip, seemed to hesitate, then began again. "It's about my job."

"Oh?" Come on, be nice to him, she told herself. He's been through enough tonight. She gave him an encouraging smile. "Where do you work, anyway?"

For a long moment, Mathieu looked into her eyes. Then he broke off his gaze and focused on the floor.

"Here and there."

"Huh?"

"That is, I work freelance, so I go around to lots of places—the offices of my clients. I'm a freelance IT consultant."

"That's your confession? I've heard worse!" Léa laughed.

"Well, what I wanted to tell you is … because I'm a freelancer, I often work until late at night and don't have time to cook. Since meat is all I know, I haven't been able to change my diet yet. I usually cook a big piece of meat around the beginning of the week, so I can quickly grab a few slices from the fridge each night after work. I wanted to explain this at the supermarket yesterday, but there wasn't a chance."

"I'm sorry. I guess it didn't help that I was practically yelling at you. I suppose I've been on edge lately. But why did you even say you were vegetarian in the first place? I was just telling Julien that it's all about progress, not perfection."

"If you only knew how much I regret it! I came here the first time to get a better idea about this kind of food. Then I saw you … and I guess I thought a vegetarian guy would seem more appealing than a carnivore trying to become flexitarian."

"I see." Another example of the primitive male brain at work, she thought with a smile. "But as I was saying at the supermarket, I have no problem being friends with omnivores."

"Actually, Léa, I have something more than friendship in mind."

Oh! What was this?

He came back up to the top step and took her hand. "That is, if you can ever forgive me someday."

Perhaps more caution was required, but her sophisticated female brain refused to cooperate. The feeling of his fingers on her palm had paralyzed the cerebral circuits responsible for her earlier misgivings. Sure, he had misrepresented himself, but she didn't sense anything insincere about the way he was looking at her now, and she was touched that he had come back to explain. Her heart beat faster, and a feeling of warmth that she had almost forgotten altogether began to spread through her body.

Twenty-one

Around ten o'clock, Mathieu entered his office, his head still buzzing with a kind of euphoria. What a night! The memory of his lovemaking with Léa, very fresh in his mind, was so different from what he'd felt two days before, with Astrid. The images replaying were softer, more delicate, as if enveloped by a mysterious halo of light. What had happened? Had Léa awakened in him a new feeling he had never suspected was possible?

The phone rang. It was the advertising agency. The creative director enthusiastically informed him that one of their ideas for Nedelec Pork's next product launch, jellied ham with parsley, was to use the vegetarians as a target. It was a TV spot that would show a sad teenage boy who had been fed lettuce all his life, as if he were a snail. The poor lad would manage to convince his eco-hippie-veggie parents to take him to a supermarket where he would taste a sample of Nedelec Pork jellied ham. It would be a eureka moment in which he renounced fruits and vegetables forever. "A biting satire of the vegetarian lifestyle," concluded the creative director.

Mathieu wanted to tear his hair out. "I don't know if that's a good idea. Especially right now. To be honest, I'd prefer something less controversial."

He hung up. The call had brought him back to reality. The day before, he would have thought the ad was a great idea, but today it was different. Today, everything was different.

What had he been thinking? Would he even be able to see Léa again? After all, he had knotted the noose around his own neck when he'd lost his nerve and left out the key part of his confession: his job at this cursed company! And to make matters worse, he was supposed to be in a very serious relationship with Astrid. If Arlette hadn't been in the next room, he would have gladly tested the resistance of his office walls with his head. Instead, he collapsed into his chair.

Just then, Arlette, seated at her desk, let out a muffled yelp of surprise. Mathieu had to pinch himself to believe it: A human shape had just burst through the door and was heading straight for him. Its heels made a sound like gunshots as it marched across the floor, and its eyes shot out vengeful lightning bolts. Without giving him a chance to react, the intruder raised a hand.

Smack! Whack!

His head flew first in one direction, then in the other. When it came back to the center, the office was empty. He dragged himself to the window and, a few moments later, saw his attacker cross the parking lot, get into her car, and slam the door.

"Wasn't that Léa Rystel?"

Arlette's question pulled him out of his state of shock. Yes, that was Léa, in the flesh, muscles, and tendons. That was some right hook! He rubbed his cheek. And her backhand wasn't bad either.

How had she found him out? Had he talked about Nedelec brand galantine, head cheese, or Morteau sausage in his sleep? But what did it matter at this point? As all the good management textbooks said, the key was to focus on the here and now, to save his career. As long as she stayed calm and didn't set off a bomb in the parking lot, he could still get through this. Indeed, by some lucky chance, nobody had witnessed the scene.

Nobody except Arlette. He contemplated his secretary's shocked face.

"Arlette, you don't have anything to tell me about your relations with the vegetarians, by any chance? Or with Léa?"

"No."

"Are you sure?" he asked, raising his voice.

She wrung her hands in distress. "Well, actually, I may have mentioned your pork museum to her. But nothing about you! I didn't say anything about you!" Her lips trembled. "I was afraid to tell you, but I gave my notice this morning."

"What!"

"I don't want to participate in this criminal industry any longer."

Criminal! Just listen to that! He should have given her a stern reprimanding, but he didn't have the heart for it. He managed a small smile. "Relax. Just promise me you'll say nothing about what you just saw. Okay?"

"Don't worry."

But he was worried. Even sick with anxiety. This night with Léa, a sort of truce between enemy troops, had been a unique experience: love—for that's what it was, he realized—was no longer such a mystery to him. But the fighting had just resumed, and his dislocated jaw reminded him very clearly which side he was on.

In any case, he tried to console himself, it was better this way. He couldn't imagine going vegetarian: holding the fate of the world at the end of his fork at every meal, seeing dietary conspiracies everywhere he looked, ranting for hours about the suffering of a lobster plunged into a pot of boiling water, or raving over a dish of cumin-seasoned sprouted lentils—it was all beyond his powers. The heart may have its reasons of which reason knows nothing, as the old adage said, but the stomach of an omnivore did, too—his in particular.

And this also solved the problem of Astrid. There was no reason now not to keep seeing her, and he had to remember that she could do wonders for his career. To make up for the canceled dinner, he would invite her to go on a little trip this weekend.

Yet somehow, these thoughts couldn't keep him from falling into a very black mood.

Twenty-two

Although her palm stung, Léa regretted not hitting him harder. She was still in shock from the phone call she'd received that morning from a friend in the vegetarian society who had suspicions about Mathieu. After that, confirming that this so-called IT consultant was in reality the mastermind of Nedelec Pork's marketing strategy was easy enough. To think that she had just slept with the very man who was trying to ruin her business so he could open a museum glorifying the killing of pigs! But she hadn't expected to see Arlette working alongside him. During her confession about the museum at La Dame Verte, Arlette had never mentioned this monster's name!

Léa had long sensed that Mathieu wasn't completely forthright, but she'd never suspected anything like this. How she would have liked to erase her night with him, to eradicate it from her mind! But the memory of his hands still lingered on her body, the taste of his lips remained on her own, the scent of his cologne still titillated her nostrils, and this fierce struggle between thoughts and sensations left her spent and disoriented.

She turned the key in the ignition and stepped down hard on the gas pedal. The worst of it was that despite its role in sending hundreds of animals to their deaths every day, Nedelec Pork had the same calm, clean, and respectable appearance as any other company. The figures were enough to chill your blood. Twenty-five million pigs slaughtered every year in France—that was nearly seventy thousand daily executions that, despite the cruelty of it, took place to the almost unanimous indifference of the general public. Not to mention the five million cattle, forty million rabbits, and nine hundred seventeen million chickens, ducks, turkeys, guinea fowl, and geese.

But if Mathieu hoped she would close down La Dame Verte, he could think again. Léa would die before she made room for his rotten museum. In fact, she would show that blood drinker that vegetarians didn't have turnip juice running through their veins.

Back at the restaurant, the sight of Pervenche sitting on the front steps did nothing to improve her mood. What did that troublemaker want now? Was she going to threaten to sue her for unfair dismissal? Treat her to one of the moralizing lectures she was so good at? These thoughts gave way to surprise when she saw that her ex-employee was tongue-tied.

"A huge sankhara came to me in my meditation this morning, and I realized that I've been intolerant toward you."

Léa unclenched her fists. "Don't say that."

"No, it's true. Vegetarians, vegans—we're all in the same boat. Even in our carnivore cousins, there exists a seed of goodness and wisdom. It's up to us to make it grow. If you take me back, I will never again criticize your decisions. That's a promise."

Léa was stupefied. She had never taken Pervenche's spirituality and meditations seriously, but the girl had just forgiven her for firing her in the heat of the moment, had come back to offer her services, and was proposing a universal *pax alimentaria,* which, although utopic, was generous nonetheless. If Léa weren't so uptight, she would have hugged her.

"Me, too. I was unfair to you. Listen, I don't know how much longer this ship will be afloat, but I'd be happy to have you with me while it lasts. Let's go inside."

They worked the lunch service together, and then Léa went up to her apartment in a pensive mood. Under Pervenche's peace-making influence, she was inclined to rethink her judgment of Mathieu, their "carnivore cousin." After all, it wouldn't be the first time that the circumstances of life, the pressures of society, or the weight of hierarchy would lead someone to commit acts exceeding the bounds of their natural capacity for harm. And come to think of it, given his strange "confession" of the night before, maybe he had even intended to tell her the real truth.

But the sight of her rumpled bed sheets, the imprints left by their bodies still visible, brought all of her anger rushing back. That asshole! The hurt was so deep it became a physical pain. She grabbed the phone, dialed a number, and left a message:

"Hi Max, this is Léa. I'd like to talk some more about the video you're planning to make at the pig farm."

Twenty-three

Mathieu grabbed hold of the pummel on his saddle to keep from falling, swearing between his teeth. For him, this horseback riding session was literally a pain in the rear end, but Astrid was galloping ten yards ahead of him, chirping with happiness. The castle resort where he had taken her for the weekend had its own stables, and she hadn't been able to resist the temptation to jump on a horse and meander along the beaches. The sunny weather was perfect for it, and he didn't want to say no to anything she asked, especially after his deplorable, regrettable misstep with Léa. Luckily, Astrid hadn't found out. She was still cooking up a cushy career for him and was insisting on meeting his mother and stepfather when they visited the following weekend.

He began wondering what gift he could get for her to show his commitment. Since she was the kind of woman who would interpret a bouquet of flowers on Valentine's Day as a declaration of love and a precious stone as an eternal vow, one of these conventional gifts would do. He'd look for a ring. Perhaps it was superficial, but after all, he wasn't the most original guy.

Yet when he compared Astrid to Léa, which he did about every twenty seconds on average, the gulf dividing them made him dizzy. People who marched to the beat of a different drum were sociopaths, according to Astrid, while Léa couldn't abide the nine-to-five lifestyle. One was addicted to shopping, and the other wanted to abolish their consumer society. The heiress of Nedelec Pork was looking for a stud to ensure her posterity, while the woman behind La Dame Verte sought a companion with whom to share her existential concerns. Existential concerns? That was the problem. He was just as incapable of having those as he was of having deep feelings. The awareness of his own uselessness—his belonging to this gray and shapeless mass of people who would never interest Léa—squashed his morale.

After making their way along the Trédrez cliffs, they could see the Pointe d'Armorique. They crossed a stretch of land strewn with colorful touches of heather and gorse. Astrid turned her mare onto a path leading down a bank, and they found themselves on the beach of Saint-Michel-en-Grève, the destination of their jaunt. The fifteenth-century church that rose up facing the sea was beautiful, but a strange and nauseating smell filled the hot air.

"Over there!" shouted Astrid, galloping off toward the shore.

Mathieu's old nag followed them. Under the *clop-clop* of hooves, the hard sand gave way to a carpet of increasingly thick seaweed. Soon the horses slowed and came to a stop.

His thighs burning from the friction against the saddle, Mathieu straightened up, grimacing. Although the sea was only a stone's throw away, its pleasant scent was covered by the stink of rotten eggs. His mount tapped a foot and folded back her ears. Mathieu saw Astrid, ahead of him, lift her riding crop and whack it against the flank of her mare, whose hooves were sinking deeper into the seaweed. A horn sounded. Turning his head, Mathieu saw a yellow tractor-like vehicle that looked as if it belonged on a construction site, with a shovel on the front and a hoe on the back. When he looked over at Astrid again, her mare was nowhere to be seen, and Astrid was lying on a mound of seaweed.

He got down from his horse and grabbed Astrid under the arms while his nag whinnied and made a run for it. What was happening? His sense of smell seemed anesthetized, and he was growing faint. He, too, fell down onto the green magma just as a voluminous shape blocked the sun. It was the loading shovel of the vehicle that had come to rescue them. A man in blue coveralls and a mask helped them get inside the glassed-in cab.

"That damned seaweed!" the man exclaimed, removing his mask and driving down the beach at top speed. "A little longer and you'd have been done for!"

Leaning out the window, Astrid vomited her lunch of poached haddock and braised leeks. His eyes burning, Mathieu noticed the horses galloping behind them. The driver, who seemed to be in his sixties, continued to explain, shouting to be heard over the noise from the engine.

"It's because of the hydrogen sulfide. Ten years ago, a jogger died at that very same spot. Several of my coworkers have fallen into comas. We work for the city and have been removing that deadly seaweed by the ton, but it doesn't make much difference. It's full of sulfur, so when it decomposes, it releases a toxic gas." He shook his head with a look of disgust. Then, turning toward Astrid, he asked, "Do you want to see a doctor?"

"Thank you, but I'll be okay."

Killer seaweed! What in the world? Mathieu hadn't felt this weak in a long time. A few moments later, the backhoe loader came to a stop on the dry sand just in front of the church, and the driver helped them get out. As a few onlookers watched, Mathieu and Astrid retrieved their horses and drank from a bottle of mineral water Astrid had with her. She was getting her color back quickly, and, unlike him, jumped back on the saddle with no trouble.

"We really owe you one!" she said to their savior as he was about to leave.

"Don't mention it."

She contemplated the sunny beach. "Such a lovely spot. What a shame!"

The man shrugged his shoulders. "It's the fault of those pork producers."

"What?"

"The seaweed proliferates like that because of the nitrates from the hog manure they spread over the fields." He drove the toe of his boot into the sand angrily. "This is what happens when you protect intensive livestock production at all costs!"

Now it was Mathieu who wanted to rescue the man—from Astrid's wrath. Did he realize what he was saying? And to whom he was saying it?

Indeed, his companion's reaction was not long in coming. "Do you have proof for what you claim?"

Mathieu was unable to prevent the bad turn the conversation was about to take. After exchanging a few terse words with the man, Astrid rose up on her stirrups, red with fury.

"You're talking nonsense!"

The driver brandished his fist. "If you keep on like that, I'm going to regret pulling you out of there!"

The onlookers applauded. Beside herself with rage, Astrid looked at Mathieu, who wanted only a hot shower and would gladly have avoided all of this fuss.

"That's nothing but shameless environmentalist propaganda—a pack of lies!" Astrid shouted as she turned her horse back. "Let's go! We don't need to stick around here!"

On the way back, Mathieu replayed the incident in his mind. Was there really a connection between spreading pig manure in the fields, its infiltration into the groundwater, and the proliferation of that repugnant seaweed? And, more generally speaking, was the meat industry really responsible for all the things it was accused of? He played the devil's advocate out of pure masochism. If you compared them to arms dealers or financial speculators, meat manufacturers were as innocent as lambs. And if he didn't do this work, someone else would. His role in society was not to change the world but to maximize the profits of his company. But was this noble mission a personal choice? Or, as with his relationships, an external imposition that he'd internalized by default?

They slept for ten hours in a row and spent part of the following day lounging in the resort's pool area. Astrid didn't make the slightest allusion to their misadventure of the day before. She put on an alluring outfit for dinner. Back in their room afterward, she wanted Mathieu to make love to her, but there was another unfortunate incident: His equipment wouldn't cooperate.

"It's because of yesterday," he mumbled. "The jolting against the saddle … "

She readjusted her filmy lingerie bitterly.

"Your nose usually *grows* when you lie."

Should he interpret this sexual allusion, which was in very poor taste by the way, as a sign that she was onto him? And what was happening to his sacrosanct virility? This was the first time it had let him down, although he would need a calculator to work out the number of women he'd slept with. Jolting against the saddle—what a pathetic excuse!

Later, in the dark, he wondered why his liaisons with women so often ended this way: him lying there with his arms crossed next to a sleeping woman he felt ambivalent about. Was he a kind of boy-toy who let himself be seduced out of fear of experiencing real feelings? Did he desire the women, or was he afraid of what they could reveal to him about himself? Was he agreeing to be a sex object for lack of anything better, since he hadn't yet had the chance to be the protagonist in his own romance? Léa flashed into his mind yet again, which depressed him even more.

Twenty-four

Where had she gone? Had something happened to her?

Wearing boots and a black ski jacket, Léa shone the beam of her flashlight on a bush, calling Charline's name at the top of her lungs. The sound of an engine in the night was the only response. No trace of the miniature pig, and Léa had already gone through the area around La Dame Verte with a fine-toothed comb.

She suppressed an urge to cry and noted that the noise of the engine was growing louder. Was it already eleven o'clock? In her distress, she had almost forgotten that Max and his friends would be coming by to pick her up. What would she tell them? With Charline missing, she didn't feel up to participating in the mission anymore.

A moment later, big yellow headlights turned the corner, and an old van came to a stop in front of La Dame Verte. Max, sitting in the passenger seat, was holding Charline on his lap.

"It's lucky this hunk of iron won't go faster than forty miles an hour, or we might have run her over!" he joked.

Léa felt her heart melt.

"Charline! Never do that again, okay?" She wiped away a tear. "Where did you find her?"

"She was hitchhiking about two miles from here," said the guy at the wheel. "I'm sorry, Léa, but we have to get going."

"We can bring her, if you want," suggested Max, patting the little pig.

It wasn't only that Léa didn't have the heart to lock the absconder up at home. She also felt the need to hold her close.

"Are you sure? She's not fully housebroken yet, after all."

"Don't worry! These seats have seen worse," said a third voice from the back of the van.

They made their way through a suburb of Rennes, got onto a national freeway, then pulled off onto a country road. Between the black hedges, Léa could see phantom-like fields and, in the distance, shreds of sky with disturbing shapes. Hugging Charline tight, Léa thought back to her teenage years, when she had run away from home at night a few times. She now re-experienced the same feeling of danger, of the unknown, the same rapid heartbeat. At length, the hedges gave way to a fence that revealed a low, rectangular building with a tiled roof topped with dark towers. Silos, Léa thought.

"Here we are," Max announced. "The Nedelec pig farm."

He parked the van on the side of the road. Before they got out, Max briefed everyone on their respective missions. His wire cutters and crowbar would get them into the building. His friends would operate the night-vision camera and audio-recording equipment while Léa narrated the visit.

Léa pulled her script out of her pocket. She could have volunteered to take care of the lighting or to serve as the lookout, but she wanted to be the one on camera, so Mathieu and his accomplices at Nedelec Pork would go rabid with fury when they saw her on YouTube. She also hoped her task would distract her from what they would see inside.

They left Charline in the van and climbed over the fence.

Léa's pulse was racing. Seeing videos online was one thing, but confronting the reality of it was altogether different. Grunting sounds pierced through the blackness. What had she gotten herself into this time?

Max forced the door open with his crowbar, and the smell of ammonia hit Léa like a kick in the stomach. Taking a handkerchief from her pocket and holding it over her nose, she looked through the door. She could just make out the building's interior structure and some large shapes moving around in the dark near the floor.

"This is the fattening room," explained Max. "When they reach around two hundred forty pounds, it's off to the slaughterhouse for them. You okay, Léa?"

No, not really. She knew she was as pale as the backs of the hundreds of pigs crammed into that room, fated to gain that unimaginable amount of weight in just five months.

"If you prefer, we can do the tour first, and you can read your script afterward."

She nodded.

"Okay," said Max, turning to his friends. "Start filming."

Léa saw that some of the animals had sores oozing pus on various parts of their bodies. Max noticed her gaze. "They'll end up on dinner plates all the same," he said.

Revolting. But it didn't surprise her. She'd never really believed in the fairy tale of the slice of healthy, tender ham from a happy pig.

They made their way through the building to the weaning room, which reminded her of the part in her script about the treatment piglets received soon after birth: Their teeth were filed down, their tails were docked, and then, once they reached sixteen pounds, they were transferred from the so-called "maternity room" to the fattening room, where they were fattened up over several months on slatted flooring, a dangerous and slippery metal mesh. To prevent the stress caused by weaning, antibiotics were mixed into their food, which was composed mainly of soy. Léa's eyes settled on a piglet who was trembling.

"It's because of the castration," explained Max. "They do it without any anesthesia."

In the next stall, another piglet whimpered as it struggled to free a hoof that had become caught in the flooring. Léa crossed the barrier and helped it. In the depth of this peaceful night in Brittany, not far from sleepy, thatched-roof houses, in this antechamber of death and perpetual insomnia that intensive livestock operations were, she felt the same visceral fear that the animals did. Max quickly led them to another room, where the snouts of enormous sows, swollen from continually pressing against the bars, peeked out from cages lined up along the wall.

"Is this the maternity room?" asked Léa, shaking a bit.

Their flashlight brought the sows out of their lethargy, and they began biting the bars of their cages. The group stopped in front of a stall divided in two: A sow was on one side, while her litter of piglets was on the other, suckling through the bars that separated them. Max told the cameraman to film them, then pointed out a small motionless shape in the sow's cage—a dead piglet.

Another line from her script came to Léa's mind: "The space is so small that a sow will sometimes crush one of her babies as they nurse, which causes her even more stress. For this reason, they are kept in separate cages, although very small piglets sometimes manage to squeeze through."

What depravity made them call that a "maternity room"? Where was the gentleness of a maternity room in these cages that were so small the mothers could not even turn around and often developed serious neurological disorders? Wasn't this more like a torture chamber?

Léa felt something else rise up inside her that was stronger than her fear: indignation—an indignation that transcended vegetarianism, omnivorism, and carnivorism. It was simply a human indignation. If people like Mathieu didn't want to see this suffering, she would force them to look. She turned to Max.

"I think I'm ready."

Once they had all the footage they needed for their documentary, they headed back toward the van. Everything had gone as they'd hoped, and the video would be on YouTube in a few hours' time. But the darkness of the night suddenly flashed into brightness, and they found themselves encircled by men in uniform. Max exploded into a volley of curses while Léa, dumbfounded, noticed a police car parked a short distance away. An officer shone his light through a window of the van and onto Charline, who was jumping up against the glass.

"You say you're vegetarians, but then you steal some ribs for a barbecue, huh?"

Deaf to Léa's protests, he opened the door, and Charline, who was always ready to make a run for it, disappeared into the night.

It was almost eleven o'clock in the morning, and some thirty people, including a few news reporters bristling with microphones and cameras, were waiting on the other side of the police station door. When she saw them, Léa stepped back and turned toward her attorney.

"Let me handle this," he said.

He descended the steps as several cameras clicked and flashed. Norbert, with the assistance of the national French Vegetarian Society, had succeeded in getting the media involved and hiring an attorney, but Léa was too worried about Charline to make any public statements. She now knew firsthand the pain people experience when their animal companions go missing. It was proof that people attributed feelings to their pets and considered them able to experience emotions at least as strong as, if not stronger than, those of human beings.

A reporter asked the first question, and the attorney hastened to answer. "The only reasonable solution was to free my client. It would have been scandalous to leave her in police custody when we have evidence that Nedelec Pork has been harassing her to get her to close her restaurant."

"Did she hit the officer?"

"She was about to but held back, which is very different. Especially since the officer has admitted that he intentionally provoked her."

It wasn't true. She really *had* slapped the cop responsible for Charline's escape, and this was why she'd been held at the station after Max and the others were released in the middle of the night. The attorney continued his performance.

"There was no reason for her to be held, unless it was the lobbying of the meat producers and their determination to silence the vegetarians. My client and her companions were only trying to denounce the scandalous conditions at local hog farms."

A boom microphone swung around the attorney and came to a halt under Léa's nose. A camera zoomed in on her. "Ms. Rystel, do you have anything to add?"

"Yes. I encourage all consumers to ask for a tour of an industrial pig farm to see the conditions for themselves."

"Isn't that a little extreme?"

"I have always promoted a culinary approach to vegetarianism, but we cannot hide behind our ignorance of the meat manufacturers' practices."

"But Nedelec Pork certifies that its facilities comply with all the standards."

She stared into the camera and could almost see Mathieu watching her at the other end, hanging on her every word. Was he really so clueless, so conventional, so cowardly? When it came to love, she knew she was too impulsive, too romantic, too quick to use instinct and intuition to separate the wheat from the chaff. She'd entered relationships with the wrong kind of man time and time again, and none of her romances had lasted very long. Yet a man whose eyes filled with tears after making love couldn't be all bad. But that made him all the more unforgivable.

"Pfft! I know their marketing director very well, and I can assure you that he lies as easily as he breathes. If their farms were up to standard, do you think they would go to such lengths to get their hands on the footage we shot?"

The reporter seemed surprised. "Is it as bad as all that?"

"Ask to see it for yourself."

Twenty-five

Bam! On the verge of a stroke, Auguste retrieved his fingers from the desktop and called the crisis-unit meeting to order. "Okay, kids, you know what we have to do now!" He took the memory card containing the footage shot at the pig farm and dropped it into the porcelain piggy bank. "Those terrorists won't come to look for it here, at least."

Mathieu fidgeted with the knot of his tie. Ever since Léa had made those statements on television, the tension had been as thick as split-pea soup. She had placed him on an ejection seat—his favor with Auguste was at its lowest point ever. Not to mention the collateral damage: It would now be impossible to touch even a hair on La Dame Verte's head without attracting the ire of journalists from both the local and national media.

He left the office, followed by Astrid and Jean-Sylvain, who couldn't resist taking a dig at him. "I hope you won't disappoint us like you disappointed Léa Rystel."

"I've already explained what that was about!"

"Calm down! I was only joking," replied Jean-Sylvain before heading for the door.

Mathieu clenched his fists and looked for support in Astrid's eyes, but in vain. "You don't believe me either?" He resumed his line of defense. "She only said that to stir up trouble among us. We met only a few times, and I've never fraternized with the vegetarians in any way!"

"That's not what scares me." Her eyes, encircled with a thick coat of mascara, grew misty. "Do you promise me that you've never—"

"Astrid!" Had he forgotten how jealous she was? He took her in his arms and felt her relax.

"Oh, sweetie, I'm sorry. I know there was never anything between you and that horrible anorexic girl."

Mathieu felt his face burning. Lately, his sexual performance with her left much to be desired. He sighed. "Calm down. We're all on edge. It's normal."

"Yes, you're right." She pulled away. "You'd better go. We have a lot to do."

In an effort to put a halt to the media frenzy, it had been decided that they would hold a tour of the swine confinement buildings for journalists. Astrid would contact them while Mathieu went to the farm to supervise a minor makeover (this task had originally been assigned to Jean-Sylvain, but the jerk had weaseled out of it).

Yet, rather than going straight to the farm, Mathieu made a stop at the jeweler's to pick up the ring that he'd ordered for Astrid the day before. The thought that this miniscule, somewhat glittery object cost the same as a luxury sedan made him feel sick. He hastily shoved the velvet box into his pocket, earning himself a look of disapproval from the saleswoman. He returned to his car. Overcome with a sense of foreboding, he plugged in his GPS—he didn't know the way to the farm.

As he approached, the silos rising up in the distance against the gray sky made him shiver. What a gloomy place.

Several vans and a big truck were parked near the swine building, where a team of workers was renovating the façade. The foreman gave him a report: A second team was at work cleaning the inside, and everything was going according to schedule. Motioning to the truck, he added that the sick animals, the ones that had to be kept away from the cameras, would be evacuated in a few minutes' time. He then pointed to the entrance of the building.

"Would you like to have a look?"

Mathieu had read that industrial hog operations were crawling with viruses. He certainly had no desire for one of those bugs, which were supposedly able to decimate many millions of people, to latch onto him. But then he thought of Léa, who, without saying as much, had challenged him to go through that door.

"Hmm … okay."

When he came back out, the trembling in his legs forced him to lean against a wall for support. An existential doubt came over him: Did this difficulty he'd felt in witnessing the animals' suffering mean that he would be unable to kill an animal? If so, he couldn't rule out the possibility that he belonged to a sub-category of carnivores, a second and less glamorous division that included hyenas, vultures, and other scavengers. Disturbed by this realization, he stepped away from the truck into which the workers were beginning to load the sick pigs.

His cell phone rang. His mother wanted to know whether Astrid would be coming with him to meet them at the train station the next day.

"Uh … yes, Mom, of course."

Snort, oiiiiink, snort, snort.

"Mathieu, dear, what's going on?"

"Nothing, nothing."

Frantic squeals were coming from the area around the

truck. Mathieu looked and saw a worker carrying a black piglet over to the foreman. Intrigued, Mathieu moved closer, still holding the phone to his ear.

"I'm so proud of you," said his mother. "If you knew how we've worried about you ever since you left for Rennes!"

That he could very well imagine. Henri had undoubtedly predicted a thousand catastrophes linked to his allegedly unstable nature. Rising to the position of general manager through a princely marriage to Astrid would have been an excellent way to shut his stepfather up for good, but now he'd gone and jeopardized everything with a treasonous affair. Could he still salvage the situation? Perhaps, but only if he made no more mistakes.

"D'you think we're the Humane Society or something?" the foreman shouted to the worker. "Put that in the truck, on the double!"

Damn! Those little black feet, that quivering snout … it could only be Léa's miniature pig. What the hell was it doing here? He ended the call with his mother and glared at Charline. Did she realize the situation she'd put him in? Oh, she could look at him with those imploring little eyes all she wanted—he wasn't going to cave. For that matter, since she supposedly had a high level of intelligence, had she ever reflected upon the difference between a just cause and a good cause? Fighting climate change seemed just, for example, but the Kyoto Protocol, which would have destroyed a million jobs in the United States alone, was a bad cause. Vegetarianism also seemed just, but the end of the meat industry would increase unemployment as surely as any intervention on his part in the next few seconds would put an end to his career at Nedelec Pork once and for all.

Oh yes, the world was a terribly complex place. Seeing things in black and white, or green and red, was something for dreamers or idealists with dangerous views. And so he wouldn't lift a finger for Charline. Nope. Sorry. He turned away from the truck that would, in a few minutes' time, head straight for the slaughterhouse.

Twenty-six

Léa rushed over to the ringing telephone in the hope of hearing news of Charline.

"Hello?" said a voice on the other end. "I'd like to make a dinner reservation. Do you have any tables left?"

Instead of jumping for joy—they would be fully booked that night, which had never before happened—she felt the lump in her throat growing tighter. Almost a whole week had gone by since Charline's disappearance. Her searches through the area around the pig farm having yielded nothing, she had to prepare herself for the worst.

"Of course. How many in your party?" she asked, forcing herself to sound friendly.

Noting the answer down into her reservation book, she looked around the dining room nervously. It needed a sweeping, and half the tables were still not set. In the kitchen, things were not much better. It was true that her recipe for Asturian beans with diced turnip and carrot, topped with fresh wakame mixed with tarragon and a pumpkinseed oil and spirulina cream, which was delicious in spite of its strange name, required a great deal of skill and endless patience, especially since Pervenche was unable to make the simplest emulsion.

"Did it work this time?" she asked her assistant as she entered the kitchen, where two huge pots of beans were bubbling away.

Pervenche wiped her hands on her apron. "No," she replied grumpily. "There must be something missing from your recipe. This wouldn't happen otherwise. I never mess up a mayonnaise."

"Mayonnaise? I thought you didn't eat eggs anymore."

"I was talking about *vegan* mayonnaise," retorted Pervenche. "Soy milk can easily be used instead of eggs. It's cheaper, better for the animals, and even has the same taste as egg mayo, if you want to know the truth."

"This reminds me of another conversation we once had," grumbled Léa, taking the electric mixer from her. "I'll do it. If you could just finish setting the tables, that would be great."

"You're the boss."

Léa clenched her teeth. Pervenche seemed to have forgotten her promise to never again criticize Léa's decisions or her fondness for eggs and cheese. As for Pervenche's passive-aggressive tendency, it was getting worse before Léa's eyes. How naive she'd been to think that people could change!

She combined the goat's milk yogurt, spirulina, toasted pumpkinseed oil, and umeboshi juice in a large bowl and already felt calmer. Making emulsions was her specialty; somehow, the knowledge that an egg yolk, mustard, and oil, correctly mixed, always resulted in a good mayonnaise brought her a sense of comfort that she otherwise rarely experienced in her day-to-day life. But now, even though things were going well, it was for the wrong reason. She was sure that the people of Rennes were rushing to La Dame Verte just to get a look at her, after her appearance on television following her arrest, rather than to taste her food. But given the state of her bank account, she certainly couldn't afford to turn anyone away. She started up her mixer and watched the ingredients melt into a smooth, creamy texture with a delicate, acidic scent.

~

That night, at one o'clock, she closed the shutters on her bedroom window and was about to try to get some sleep when a familiar sound rose up from the street.

Snort, oiiiiink, snort, snort.

She had to pinch herself to believe it. As the grunting continued, she shoved her arms into a bathrobe, flew down the stairs, crossed the dining room in a flash, and unlocked the front door. Charline rushed against her legs, squirming with happiness. A long piece of twine knotted loosely around her neck was tied to one of the ground-floor window shutters.

Léa kissed her joyfully, then squinted into the blackness between the halos from the streetlights. Nobody.

A chaos of thoughts and feelings came over her as she untied the little adventurer. Her intuition told her that Mathieu had something to do with this reappearance. One way or another, Charline must have taken refuge in the Nedelec pig building, and Mathieu was the only one who could have made the connection between Charline and Léa.

Snapshots from the night she and Mathieu had spent together came back to Léa in sweet waves, and a slight shiver ran over her skin. Meeting a man who knew the importance of foreplay and didn't confuse the act of love with bodybuilding was a rare thing these days.

But if he thought he could get back on her good side, he was dead wrong. The softness of his hands was matched only by the perverseness of his mind. Moreover, Pervenche had already demonstrated that a person's nature was unchangeable. An animal-eating pathological liar would always be an animal-eating pathological liar.

But an inner voice protested. Okay, all men were bastards, but given that he'd brought Charline back to her, shouldn't she cut him a little slack? Since we are what we eat, if Mathieu were to reduce his meat intake, he would surely only improve with time.

But after what she'd seen in the pig building, Léa didn't know whether she would really be able to share her life with a carnivore, even with separate refrigerators. She took Charline under her arm and went inside to prepare her a bottle.

Twenty-seven

Pacing back and forth in the entrance hall of the Rennes train station, Mathieu no longer knew which of the two women, or which diet, corresponded best to his feelings and beliefs. And how had he managed to get not only on Léa's bad side but Astrid's, too?

As the arrival of the train from Paris was announced, he trudged toward the platform with leaden feet. When his mother and stepfather emerged from the train, he had to suppress an urge to run for the hills. Kissing him on the cheek, his mother made no effort to hide her disappointment.

"You're on your own?"

"Astrid had something come up at the last minute. You'll see her tonight."

Henri, a man in his sixties with a large belly, a wide nose, and shifty eyes, stared at him. "You look like you have a fever."

"No, I'm fine." Incredible! He'd barely arrived, but this killjoy was already looking for something to fault him for.

Mathieu's cell phone rang. It was impossible, he knew,

but he wondered whether it could be Léa calling to thank him for returning Charline.

"Mathieu … " It was Astrid. The day before, she'd found out that he'd saved Léa's pig, and she had thrown a colossal tantrum. Pure empathy, and the widening circle of compassion, which he'd cited as the reasons for which he'd saved Charline from a certain death, had not convinced her. On the contrary, she had gone on and on about Léa and Mathieu's supposed romance, and had even refused to accompany him to the station. What was she going to add now?

"I'm sorry about this morning," she said. "I've been a bundle of nerves lately. Have your mom and stepdad arrived?"

"Yes."

"So I'll see you later at the restaurant?"

Dear Astrid! What an amazing woman. He didn't deserve her. He would henceforth be a faultless lover, an irreproachable businessman, a carnivore above all suspicion!

That evening, everyone met at La Chope Bretonne, a classy downtown brasserie. Mathieu's mother was dressed to the nines, and Astrid, decorated like a Christmas tree, made a big impression on both his mother and stepfather. So the introverted young Parisian who'd come to Rennes only a year earlier on the faith of a classified ad had, after all, achieved success beyond all expectations.

They took seats at a round table in a private room whose windows offered a superb view of the Saint Pierre cathedral. They ordered kirs for their aperitif and began studying the menu. Mathieu chose asparagus in a béchamel sauce as his starter. But for the main dish, in an effort to show Astrid that he was still faithful to the cause, he ordered the pork tenderloin with truffled potato croquettes.

His mother asked Astrid about her family, and his stepfather, after posing a few polite questions about Nedelec Pork, began speaking of the spiking prices of milk and the adverse conditions of the yogurt industry. No doubt about it, thought Mathieu, this guy suffers from a case of verbal incontinence and enlarged ego that only gets worse with age.

"Our main challenge, over the next few years, will be to keep the consumption of dairy products at the current level."

"Why?" asked Astrid.

"We're under attack from all sides by loons claiming that milk isn't good for you."

Mathieu got scared. Cow's milk was the last topic of conversation he wanted for this table. It would inevitably lead to talk of plant-based milks and vegetarianism—and that would be fatal.

He raised his kir and proposed a toast. "To Astrid, and your visit."

The clinking of glasses soon gave way to the scraping of forks and knives against plates. Without his stepfather's exasperating talk about his own son's success, Mathieu would have been able to enjoy his asparagus. But once the waiter placed his pork tenderloin on the table, his experience in the pig building came rushing back and paralyzed him. The few times in his life that he had felt guilty about eating meat, he had gotten past it by telling himself that he was not eating *a pig* but just *pig*. But this time, he clearly saw *a pig*, as if an entire pig were stretched out across his plate.

Tipsy on her burgundy, Astrid began gushing to Henri about her undying love for dairy products. "Just like that old TV commercial used to say, they're my 'friends for life.'"

"And right you are. It's the best way to prevent osteoporosis."

His tone was so smug that Mathieu couldn't hold back. "Actually, that's a point under debate."

Henri's knife froze in his creamed veal shank. "Debate?"

"About osteoporosis. It's debated."

"What's this? Suddenly you have a degree in nutrition?"

"No, but everyone's heard about the calcium paradox." Actually, he'd known nothing about that himself until Léa mentioned it. He repeated what she'd told him: The world's biggest milk consumers, the Scandinavians, also had the world's highest rate of osteoporosis.

Henri dismissed this argument with a wave of his hand.

"That's only because the Nordic countries don't get enough sunshine—without sun exposure, they can't synthesize vitamin D."

"I don't mean to contradict you, but some very serious studies have shown that dairy products acidify the body, which leads to a weakening of the bones." He tried to keep his voice calm, but he felt his blood pulsing in his temples as Mr. Know-It-All glared at him angrily, as if he were a traitor to their cause. How could this numbskull not realize that they'd never been on the same side, that Mathieu had his own personality, his own opinions—opinions that were contrary to his? He'd been putting up with this man for twenty-five years, but tonight, his mother and her entreaties be damned, he would not back down.

"I believe scientists have even spoken of a cannibalization of bone tissue," he added with an almost sadistic satisfaction.

His stepfather brandished his knife. "That's just misinformation spread by vegetarians! Gibberish invented by soy-milk drinkers! If it was up to me, I'd send all those irresponsible people to the Amazon rain forest, to show them how soy crops are causing deforestation!"

"You know very well that the soy grown there is not intended for human consumption but to feed animals raised for their meat and, indirectly, for the milk industry—while bankrupting small-time farmers and poisoning the land and water with agrochemicals. And the soy is produced in enormous quantities."

"Oh, is that right? I suppose you're going to pull out some figures?"

"Yes. The French consume an average of two hundred pounds of meat, three hundred eggs, and two hundred twenty pounds of dairy products per person, per year. That's the same as five thousand square feet of soy crops per person, for animal feed alone."

A deathly silence followed. Then Astrid rose to her feet and splashed her glass of Romanée-Conti in his face. "Try to tell me *now* that you never slept with that vegetarian slut!"

She stalked out of the room without another word. Mathieu heard shouts and the sound of chairs being jostled, and, as he parted the curtain of liquid that obstructed his view, he saw his mother apparently hyperventilating as she stared at the door through which Astrid had just disappeared.

His stepfather was the first to recover his ability to speak. "Well, now. A vegetarian!" The surprise in his eyes gave way to suspicion. "Tell me I'm dreaming. You don't really fraternize with those salad-eaters?"

Mathieu should have been mortified, but he felt nothing but a pleasant apathy. "Why not?"

This provoked an immediate reaction. "Have you lost your mind or something?"

"I never had one, according to you."

Henri threw his hands up in the air. "With the responsibilities you have? If my marketing director did that to me, I'd demote him to the switchboard!"

"Don't forget that I worked as a switchboard operator when we met, Henri," interrupted his mother, who struggled to catch her breath as she mopped Mathieu's face with a handkerchief.

"Sorry, dear, but learning that your son wants to ruin his career by following a Bugs Bunny diet … you have to realize it's a shock."

"Oh, come now! Don't confuse love with what people eat. He can very well have a vegetarian friend without having joined their cult." She tried to help her son take off his jacket. "Mathieu dear, why don't you run after Astrid and try to catch her before it's too late? She's really a charming girl."

He shook his head.

"Then at least tell me who this other woman is," she said in a teasing voice.

"Léa Rystel. She runs a vegetarian restaurant that I often eat at."

Henri threw his napkin down onto the table. "You see what I mean? He's one of them!"

Mathieu was surprised at himself. How, in the middle of this disaster, was he managing to remain so calm? Had he changed that much?

He saw his mother lean toward him with imploring eyes. "Mathieu! My roast chicken … you've always loved it so much. You would even chew the bones!"

"Mom, please, don't make this worse."

Henri straightened up in his chair. "So, you admit it!"

"What?"

"That you consider chickens as your equals!"

How was it possible to have so many assumptions, prejudices, and stereotypes? Mathieu wondered. He looked down at the pork tenderloin before him and felt in his pocket for the box containing the astronomically expensive ring he'd bought for Astrid. And then, something happened inside him. He felt a liberation, as if a weight had just lifted forever from his stomach—and his heart.

"It's true. I'm a vegetarian."

Twenty-eight

Monday morning, as he entered his office, Mathieu found Arlette digging through a drawer of her desk.

"You're the only person I'm going to miss from this company," she told him as she straightened back up and placed a photo of herself in a parachutist's harness into a box of knickknacks.

Remembering that she had received the management's authorization to shorten her advance notice and leave earlier, Mathieu felt a twinge in his heart. He really liked his secretary and didn't want to be separated from her. "You won't get rid of me that easily," he said enigmatically.

She looked at him with defiance. "I warn you, nobody can convince me to stay here even one day longer. I've chosen my camp."

Her camp—that could only be vegetarianism. But he had to admit that his own allegiance was still shaky. If he could only see Léa, talk with her for even a few minutes to solidify his beliefs! But it was unthinkable that she would forgive him. Overwhelmed by these gloomy thoughts, he asked Arlette to get a box for him as well.

"What for?"

"I'm moving to the unemployment office."

"You … you're leaving, too?"

"Yes. I no longer see vegetarians as fanatics or meat-eaters as superior beings."

Arlette's eyes shone, and she clasped her hands together in delight. "Léa! I knew it!"

"Don't remind me," he said sadly. "She hates me. You saw the way she showed it."

"Pfft! Just a love tap!" She ran a hand over her hair. "Well, it must be admitted that your behavior was unacceptable. But if women were interested only in irreproachable, upright men, the human race would disappear within three generations."

He dropped into a chair. "You really know what to say to the pre-suicidal, don't you?"

"Simple feminine objectivity." She sighed. "What a shame that the footage of the pig farm was destroyed. That would have shown those murderers, if it'd been put online."

But it hadn't been destroyed. It was in the porcelain piggy bank on Auguste's desk.

Mathieu stopped and thought. Was this an opportunity for him to redeem himself? He looked at his watch.

"What's up?" asked Arlette.

"I'd better go up there right away."

If he let her in on his plan, she was likely to remind him that adrenaline was her weakness and insist on coming along. But he wanted to act alone, and quickly. It was ten minutes to ten, and the big boss would soon arrive.

A few minutes later, with his ears peeled for any possible interruptions, he tiptoed into the holy sanctum. He carefully lifted the piggy bank and turned it upside down to dump out its contents, but only a few paper clips and old franc coins fell from the slot. He realized to his horror that the only way to get the memory card out would be to smash the symbol of the Nedelec family's success. But how? The floor was covered in carpet, and he didn't have a hammer handy. Not to mention that Auguste's secretary, a cross between a Doberman and a pit bull, would come running at the slightest sound. The click of the door handle made him jump. Turning his head, he saw Astrid looking through the crack. His legs turned to jelly, and he thought he would faint.

"Arlette told me you were here," she faltered. "If you're looking for Daddy, he won't be coming in today. He's had a heart attack."

Mathieu gasped. In spite of his new dietary beliefs, he still felt affection for the old man. "How is he?"

She came into the room and told him about Auguste's coronary bypass surgery. As he moved to face her, she saw the piggy bank in his hands.

"Hey! What're you doing with Daddy's piggy bank?"

"I was, uh … admiring it."

Astrid's worried expression transformed suddenly into rage, and she ran toward him, shouting, "You wanted to steal it, huh? Taking advantage of a poor old man while he's at the hospital! Give that back at once, you filthy traitor!"

He held it out to her. She grabbed it and raised it into the air as if to smash it on his skull—but then, to his stupefaction, she crumpled to the floor like a heap of laundry.

"Oh! Mathieu darling, don't abandon me! If you only knew how ashamed I am of how I acted in front of your family! It's only because I love you so much." She sobbed, lifting a face streaming with tears. "We'll get help. There's treatment for it, you know."

"For what?"

"Vegetarianism."

Huh? Where did she live, Planet Zorg? It would have been easy enough to go along with all this and get back in

Astrid's favor, but he was tired of his own lies and wanted more honesty in his future relationships with women.

"It's not only the vegetarianism, you know. I also have feelings for Léa Rystel."

"What?" Astrid got to her feet and, clutching the piggy bank to her chest, began screaming at him. He was trying to make a strategic retreat when she suddenly turned, placed the bank on the desk, and jumped on him, her claws unsheathed. He felt her nails dig into his neck like razor-sharp blades. She had lost her mind. She was stark staring mad, and dangerous. He pushed her back and tried to get away, but the room was large and the door too far from him. He was halfway there when he heard a swishing sound from behind. The impact— at the base of his skull—plunged him into a deep, dark hole.

Twenty-nine

Mathieu started his car and slowly drove away from downtown Rennes. He still felt some tenderness in his scalp where the stitches had been, but all in all, he had gotten out of the situation fairly unscathed. Auguste's piggy bank could have fractured his neck, but instead, the bank itself had smashed into bits.

If only the impact had helped him grasp his new dietary identity more clearly, but no, he still wasn't sure whether he was a repentant carnivore or a budding vegetarian. Over these past two weeks of self-imposed house arrest, he had made many meat-free dishes, but his creations were woefully inferior to what he'd tasted at Léa's restaurant. On the other hand, the question of his future had clearly been settled: After winding up his affairs in Rennes, the ex–future general manager of Nedelec Pork would soon be pounding the pavement in Paris, looking for a new job. He'd considered staying in Brittany, but he had to think of his physical safety.

As he was approaching the town of Laval on the national freeway, he was about to pass a long line of trucks when a car coming the other way forced him to move back behind one of them. It was transporting hogs. In the old days, back when he thought animal welfare was a thing for hippies, he would have turned his eyes away from the animals crammed into the trailer with slatted sides, or told himself that they were being taken to a day camp. But now, seeing indifference as wisdom or anti-vegetarian prejudices as independent thinking had become impossible. Already heavy, his conscience now became leaden. Realizing that he was fleeing Rennes with his tail between his legs, he pulled over to the side of the road. So the carnivores wanted him dead and Léa hated his guts? He couldn't run away just because of that.

Giving up meat and a career in a harmful industry wouldn't make his life any better if he didn't also learn to fight for the things that mattered, beginning with Léa. But how could he convince her that he was now a new man—or, to put it more simply, that he had become more truly himself— without risking another slap? He remembered the idea that had popped into his mind that past week at the supermarket. It seemed worth a shot.

The door and shutters of La Dame Verte were locked. He remembered what Léa had said about closing down at the end of the month, and a weighty sensation of guilt invaded his chest. But then he noticed a note on the door: The restaurant had moved to Rue Saint-Louis downtown!

A few minutes later, he parked his car on Rue Saint-Louis and caught sight of Léa from a distance, pulling some things out of a van. She wore an old pair of blue coveralls splotched with paint, but to him she looked like an angel. How could he have treated her the way he had? He would do anything to be with her. If she would only forgive him, heck—he was even willing to become a breatharian, converting light into food just like a plant.

He approached hesitantly as Léa struggled with a box inside the van.

"I—I could help you with that," he stammered.

She glanced over her shoulder at him but didn't seem as surprised as he expected at seeing him standing there and looking so haggard, his face covered with stubble. "Thanks, but I'd rather hurt my back."

Disheartened, he contemplated the entrance of the new La Dame Verte. With its chiseled stone walls, tiled door awning, and the large planters on either side of the front step, it certainly was impressive. He laughed nervously. "Great place. Bravo!"

"It's all thanks to you and the Nedelecs."

"To us?"

"If you hadn't tried so hard to get my site, La Dame Verte never would have gotten so much publicity, and I never could have moved to this new location. Speaking of which, I hope you'll invite me to the opening reception for your new museum."

"Actually, I've taken a distance from the pork cause."

"That still leaves you seafood, fish, and all the other kinds of meat."

"I would prefer seitan, tempeh, or tofu."

She turned away from the box to face him, a cynical smile on her lips. "I know—Arlette told me about your supposed conversion … and the breakup."

He began to panic. "Breakup?"

"With the Nedelecs. It's too bad. I'm sure you would have been a great general manager."

Whew! His beloved secretary had kept her mouth shut about Astrid. He stuck a finger in his collar. "Well … I did it for you."

"For me?"

"To prove that I'd changed." He saw her brow furrow in suspicion. "You think I'm past hope? I know I'm not a model vegetarian, but if your foie gras can be better than the real one, there's room for optimism."

165

"The vegetarian foie gras, unlike some people, doesn't pretend to be real."

"Except when it's you who serves it," he replied with a wink.

She scowled at him. "But your diet isn't even the problem!" she said, her temper rising. "The problem is you lie like a rug!"

He stared at his shoes. "Forgive me, Léa. I know I've screwed up. But I wasn't lying to you the whole time."

"No kidding?"

"Remember when I said that your cardamom and persimmon flan with the dried-fruit compote was the best dessert I'd ever had? Well, I meant it."

She could never forget that moment. During their night together, around three in the morning, they'd gotten hungry. She'd gone down to the kitchen and returned with two generous portions of cardamom flan that they savored in her bed while comparing the shapes of their belly buttons. Ah, the memories.

Léa smiled sadly. "The persimmon season is over." She turned her attention back to the van, pulling out some stainless steel containers and a chafing dish. "I'm sorry, I have to hurry because we're opening again tomorrow, so … "

"I'm going back to Paris, but first I wanted to make you an offer."

Léa stiffened.

"Don't worry—nothing of a personal nature."

"Okay then. Shoot."

"I had an idea this week. Even if your new restaurant is a hit, you'll never reach more than a limited number of people. Why don't you manufacture ready-made meals under the La Dame Verte brand? I know that vegetarians are wary of processed foods, but they're also busy like everyone else. In Belgium, the market for veg products has exploded, and we'll soon see the same thing here in France."

"That'll be the day."

"No, really! People are tired of the same old moussaka, stuffed tomatoes, and hachis parmentier. Young urban women in the middle and upper classes are just waiting for an opportunity to make the move toward vegetarianism. Especially after all of those horse-meat scandals. Consumers are losing their trust in beef producers, and by extension the meat industry as a whole."

She looked at him impatiently. "Okay, but I'm already very busy with the restaurant. And I hardly have the training to become a company director."

"I could draw you up a business plan."

"You?"

He was so sure about this idea, he realized, that he was even willing to reinvest the money from Astrid's ring into the venture. Either he knew nothing about marketing, or Léa's dishes would be a hit.

"I'm going to have a lot of free time on my hands. It would be a way for me to make up for the trouble I've caused you. At least in part," he insisted. His heart was pounding. If she refused his offer, everything was lost. But her gaze softened.

"This isn't another of your dirty tricks?"

"You can trust me—really. Don't forget, I'm eating more healthfully now."

"So?"

He grinned. "I'm getting all of those toxins out of my system. A new and improved Mathieu now stands before you. And he's available on a free trial offer. Act now—supplies won't last!"

Léa couldn't help laughing. "All right then. Draw up your plan." She sighed and shook her head in amazement. "There's truly something miraculous about vegetarianism."

Epilogue

Léa collapsed into a chair. It was the third day of the international food innovation trade fair, and the background noise from the thousands of visitors, the bright lights of the stand, and the answering of visitors' questions had exhausted her.

Her company, which had just opened a new production unit in a suburb of Rennes, struggled to keep up with the orders received. Managing this business while operating La Dame Verte, which had become the first vegetarian restaurant in France to be awarded a Michelin star, was a challenging task. But the testimonials from the people who had become vegetarians or flexitarians thanks to her prepared dishes (which Mathieu preferred to call "meal solutions") made it all worthwhile. Men and women alike, but women most of all, kept telling her that going vegetarian or reducing their meat consumption had been the easiest and most beneficial decision they had ever made. Of course, there would always be a few jerks looking for a fight—like that man, who, after bumping into Arlette, had headed straight toward Léa with a threatening expression.

"Are you Léa Rystel?" He didn't even wait for her answer. "Can you tell me that the smell of barbecued meat really doesn't make your mouth water?"

"And you, can you tell me that the smell of grilled eggplant with shallots, garlic, thyme, and Espelette pepper doesn't make you hungry?"

The guy was clearly unprepared for this answer. Apparently realizing he had no witty comeback, he frowned and turned away. Léa sighed. Why were people so sure that all vegetarians disliked the taste of meat? Seeing vegetarianism as a choice made solely out of taste preference was as simplistic as considering love, for example, to be nothing more than a combination of hormones and physical attraction.

Her thoughts turned to Mathieu. Over the past two years of perfect love, she had buried her dreams of the ideal man. An ordinary man, with his strengths and flaws, too, was much better. But her partner's irreproachable vegetarianism sometimes worried her a bit. Wasn't there a danger of relapse? Of course, she didn't sense any nostalgia or longing when he spoke of the meat products he'd previously adored, but it was impossible to know whether he'd truly overcome his old demons. She looked around for him—it was almost time to start closing the stand.

～

Mathieu was doing his customary rounds to see what the competition was up to. Whistling, he headed toward the area dedicated to gourmet foods, just next to the organic products, where they had their stand.

Suddenly he stopped dead in his tracks and had to rub his eyes. That face he saw, that guy towering over everyone in the crowd—wasn't it Auguste Nedelec? Not only that, but standing next to him was Fabrizia, the lovely Milanese woman whom he'd replaced as marketing director at Nedelec Pork. What were they doing together? And wasn't their rightful place in Hall 6, the one reserved for the meat, poultry, offal, and processed pork companies? Not wanting to run into any Nedelecs, he had steered well clear of that area.

Intrigued, he began tailing the pair at a distance. Auguste soon disappeared, but Fabrizia lingered in front of the stand of a flavored olive oil producer from Italy. Mathieu went over to say hello. Luckily, she held no resentment toward him for the past, and they congratulated each other like old fellow soldiers. She was just as alluring as ever, but he was glad to see that it had no effect on him, for he was interested in only one woman now.

"What have you been up to?" he asked.

She told him that Jean-Sylvain's first decision, once he'd been promoted to general manager, had been to bring her back as marketing director.

"And you?" she asked. "Every time I mention you to the Nedelecs, they make the gloomiest faces. What in the world did you do to them?"

He remained vague and didn't mention his new position as sales director of La Dame Verte. But, knowing she was talkative, he seized the opportunity to learn a few things.

Astrid, she told him, had married the heir of another pork manufacturing dynasty in the region and had had twins. As for Jean-Sylvain's masterful sales strategy, Mathieu had noticed, not without a certain satisfaction, that it was sending them straight into a wall. Poor Nedelecs, he thought, dinosaurs that they are, representatives of a prehistoric world that was on its last gasp while the rest of humanity advanced slowly but surely toward universal vegetarianism.

The conversation soon turned to Auguste. It hadn't escaped Mathieu's notice that although the patriarch's hair was now whiter, he had lost some thirty pounds and looked as energetic as a young man. Had he followed one of those high-protein diets that made the pounds melt away in exchange for a myriad of kidney and heart problems? After a triple bypass, that would be suicide. He asked Fabrizia, and she made a wry expression.

"On the contrary. His cardiologist told him he can never again eat meat, fish, dairy products, or eggs. Apparently that's the only way he can prevent his arteries from getting clogged again."

"What! You've got to be joking." Mathieu's mouth hung open.

"Nope! He went vegan."

Mathieu felt as if the world had turned upside down. If an incorrigible carnivore like Auguste could go vegan—even if only under threat of a scalpel—then they were truly witnessing the advent of a new era. Sooner or later, the green would prevail over the red. He took leave of Fabrizia and hurried over to share the news with Léa.

About the Author

Photo credit: Christian Maury

Armand Chauvel is a French journalist and correspondent for Spain and Portugal. Born in France to an extended family of Burgundian winemakers, he spent a large part of his childhood in Senegal and Brazil due to his father's work as a tropical agronomist.

Armand studied journalism in Paris before taking work in Portugal and later in Spain. Although his journalistic focus is the economy and the business world, Armand is also passionate about the arts. He studied painting in Lisbon as well as playwriting and scriptwriting in Paris before tackling the novel genre. He became a vegetarian in 2006 after viewing the documentary *Earthlings*, and since then has taken a growing interest in the vegan diet and philosophy.

In September 2012, Armand founded the French-language blog Vegeshopper, which explores consumerism from a vegetarian/vegan perspective and features interviews on the subject with notable individuals. Armand currently resides in Barcelona with his wife and their young son. *The Green and the Red* is his first published novel.

The author would like to extend special thanks to his friend Xavier Boutaud, without whose unconditional encouragement and support this story might never have been published.

About the Translator

Photo credit: Jon Helge Hesby

Elisabeth Lyman is from the American Midwest, where she studied French, Arabic, Spanish, and linguistics before moving to San Francisco to complete a graduate degree in teaching English as a second language. She then taught for several years before pursuing further studies in French-to-English translation and establishing herself as a freelance translator.

In 2009, Elisabeth moved to Paris and there found many new opportunities to contribute to creative and literary projects through her translation work. Already a vegetarian for several years, she was inspired by the small but vibrant vegan community in France to learn more about this way of eating and living—an exploration that led to embracing veganism and developing a passion for the culinary arts. Elisabeth now divides her time between translating, cooking, and discovering the secrets of the City of Light.

Ashland Creek Press is a small, independent publisher of books with a world view. Our mission is to publish a range of books that foster an appreciation for worlds outside our own, for nature and the animal kingdom, for the creative process, and for the ways in which we all connect. To keep up-to-date on new and forthcoming works, subscribe to our free newsletter by visiting www.AshlandCreekPress.com.

Lightning Source UK Ltd.
Milton Keynes UK
UKOW02f1706131215

'64629UK00005B/3/P